THE PELICAN SHAKESPEARE

GENERAL EDITOR ALFRED HARBAGE

THE SONNETS

WILLIAM SHAKESPEARE

THE SONNETS

EDITED BY DOUGLAS BUSH AND
ALFRED HARBAGE

PENGUIN BOOKS

Penguin Books
625 Madison Avenue
New York, New York 10022

First published in *The Pelican Shakespeare* 1961
This revised edition first published 1970
Reprinted 1972, 1974, 1977, 1978, 1979

Library of Congress catalog card number: 79-98381

Printed in the United States of America by
Kingsport Press, Inc., Kingsport, Tennessee
Set in Monotype Ehrhardt

CONTENTS

Introduction   7

The Sonnets   19

Index of First Lines   175

INTRODUCTION

Shakespeare's sonnets are an island of poetry surrounded by a barrier of icebergs and dense fog; or, in the metaphor of Sir Walter Raleigh (the modern Oxford scholar, not the poet's contemporary), they have been used like wedding cake, not to eat but to dream upon. In more prosaic terms, the sonnets, as poems, have been obscured by the huge mass of speculation, much of it uncritical or crackpot, that has grown up around the "problems" presented by the dedication and the "story" adumbrated in the text. These few pages will be concerned largely with the character of the poetry, but enough must be said to justify dismissal of the speculations as immaterial and irrelevant.

The chief external facts are these: in 1598 Francis Meres, in a roll-call of contemporary authors in his *Palladis Tamia*, mentioned a number of Shakespeare's earlier plays and also "his sugred Sonnets among his private friends"; in 1599 the piratical William Jaggard printed two of the sonnets (138 and 144) in *The Passionate Pilgrim*; and in 1609 the publisher Thomas Thorpe issued 154 sonnets entitled *Shake-speares Sonnets: Never before Imprinted*, with a dedication signed "T. T." and addressed "To the onlie begetter of these insuing sonnets Mr. W. H. . . ." Although in this period an attractive name on a title page was not a guarantee of authenticity, we have no grounds for doubting that sonnets 1–152 are Shakespeare's (the apparently alien and unrelated 153 and 154 may be a spurious appendage). But we know nothing about some other important matters.

By 1609 – when Shakespeare was near the end of his dramatic career – the main vogue of sonneteering had long passed. Sir Philip Sidney's *Astrophel and Stella* (published posthumously in 1591) had inaugurated the fashion of sonnet sequences among the Elizabethan poets, Daniel, Lodge, Drayton, Spenser, and others. None of Shakespeare's sonnets can be, or at any rate has been, dated. There has been quite unconvincing argument that all or most of them were written in or by 1589. More persuasive arguments – parallels in idea and diction (some of them rare items in the poet's vocabulary) with the narrative poems and plays – would spread the sonnets over 1593–1609 but would assign the large majority to 1593–1596.

In this period books were often published without the author's knowledge or consent, since manuscript copies circulated and multiplied and one might readily fall into a publisher's hands. Evidently the publication of the sonnets was not authorized by Shakespeare but was managed by Thomas Thorpe; and he may have followed a manuscript of the whole sequence or assembled it piecemeal from fragmentary copies. Some modern scholars have rearranged the sonnets, on either mechanical or subjective principles; these rearrangements have seldom pleased anyone except the contriver. The 1609 arrangement is unsatisfactory and strongly suspect but is the only authority we have.

General opinion divides the sonnets into two main groups, though these do not form consecutive or coherent wholes. The first comprises 1–126, which may be addressed to one young man, the poet's much loved and admired friend, his junior in years and superior in social station. Obviously the first seventeen poems – commonly if rather quaintly known as "the procreation sonnets" – are appeals to a young man to marry and circumvent mortality by perpetuating his beauty and virtue in children. This plea is perhaps not in complete harmony with sonnets 18–126, in which the poet further celebrates the young man (if it is the same one, and if the subject is always a man) and his own complete love, with more or less related themes. In sonnets 127–52, the second group, he makes a radical switch to tell of his mingled passion and loathing for a dark woman (most Elizabethan heroines were golden blondes), a forsworn wife – if one woman only is involved – who, having already had the poet as a lover, has beguiled the young man into an affair, so that the poet has encountered a double disloyalty. This brief outline passes by a number of apparent discrepancies: for example, sonnets 40–42, which reproach the young man (forgivingly, to be sure) for his as yet unexplained liaison, are followed by sonnets which carry on the earlier vein of whole-hearted eulogy, as if nothing had happened. (We do not of course know the order in which the sonnets were written – or whether we have them all.) Another element in the dramatic situation is that in sonnets 79–86 the poet is displaced in the young friend's favor by a rival poet. In general, whether the cause is fidelity to real or imagined fact or dramatic art or accidental arrangement, the sonnets have the air of being day-to-day reflections, as if the poet were living in the moment, not looking back over a closed chapter, and knowing no more than the reader of what is to come.

In contrast with the relative conventionality of the other Elizabethan sequences, this dramatic "plot" – the poet, his young friend, the rival poet, and "the dark lady" – has seemed to many critics to carry special marks of actuality, and there has been much throwing about of brains (the phrase is something of a euphemism) in the effort to identify the *dramatis personae* as figures in Shakespeare's world. One source of misguided guesswork, based on a misreading of Thorpe's dedication, was the attempt to identify Mr W. H. with the poet's friend. The leading candidates for this role were Henry Wriothesley, Earl of Southampton, to whom Shakespeare dedicated *Venus and Adonis* and *Lucrece* in 1593 and 1594, and William Herbert, third Earl of Pembroke. It is now considered probable that in his dedication Thorpe was speaking, not about the contents and "story" of the sonnets, but about the manner of their procurement; that he was – with a touch of mystification calculated to excite interest in the volume – thanking a friend, Mr W. H., for having got hold of the material. However, while the dedication drops out of the case, the two young noblemen remain candidates, Herbert apparently the favorite. But the one fact is that we know nothing, and the wise reader will ignore the whole business. The same agnostic answer must be given in regard to the dark lady and her supposed originals and to the rival poet, who has been identified with a variety of Elizabethan writers. So much for "monsters and things indigest."

But agnosticism needs to go further. We do not know if the several characters (the poet included) and their relations with one another had some basis in fact or were entirely imaginary. To say that these poems, as distinguished from most other Elizabethan sequences, have a special note of actuality and intensity is only to say that Shakespeare was a greater poet – and no one would suggest that the actuality and intensity of his major plays came from personal experience of the situations and emotions there set forth. Apart from the particular and non-poetical puzzles touched on above, there have been two main approaches to the sonnets: they have been seen as only another, and superior, literary exercise in a conventional mode, and, from the opposite pole, as an intimately confessional and profound self-revelation. To cite two names no editor can overlook, Wordsworth, writing of the sonnet form, declared "With this key Shakespeare unlocked his heart"; "If so," affirmed Browning, "the less Shakespeare he." It is best to recognize that, for poets and their readers alike, the difference between actual and imaginative experience is indefinable and meaningless, and also that Shakespeare's sonnets are, like all great poetry, at once exercises in literary form and – in a broad general sense – self-revelation. They are, to be sure, very uneven, and many are far from great.

The Italian sonnet had been inaugurated in English poetry by Sir Thomas Wyatt, whose poems, with the Earl of Surrey's, were printed in *Tottel's Miscellany* (1557). But whereas the normal Italian sonnet had two divisions, an octave and a sestet, Wyatt introduced, and Surrey developed, what is called the English or Shakespearean form (*abab cdcd efef gg*), the one used, with variations, by the Elizabethan poets generally. This form, with its three quatrains and a concluding couplet (a pattern more congenial to English because of its fuller range of rhymes), fostered a manipulation of idea and imagery different from that of the Italian. In Shakespeare's sonnets the argument normally proceeds by quatrains, each one constituting a definite step, and the summarizing couplet acquires an epigrammatic or aphoristic quality (which can be weak). Thus in the famous "When, in disgrace with Fortune and men's eyes" (29), the poet in the first quatrain bewails his own lot; in the second, contrasts that lot with other men's; in the third, thinking of his beloved friend, he rises like the lark that "sings hymns at heaven's gate"; and in the couplet his felicity is generalized in a final contrast. The same formal and logical division and progression are not quite lost even in the most explosively emotional utterances, such as "What potions have I drunk of Siren tears" (119), "Th' expense of spirit in a waste of shame" (129), or "Poor soul, the center of my sinful earth" (146). If to the reader of more freewheeling modern poetry such logical formalism suggests artifice and insincerity, he forgets the rigorous training in rhetoric, given to every Elizabethan schoolboy, which made such processes of thought and feeling instinctive. The same schoolroom training, the handbooks of rhetoric, and mature poetic practise ensured the systematic knowledge and use of all kinds of verbal figures, patterns of both phrase and sound. Renaissance poets (and their readers) preferred, to borrow Robert Frost's phrase, to play tennis with a net.

Shakespeare, even more than most Elizabethan writers, thinks and feels in images, and his imagery is no less notable for control than for fecundity. The material of his images, like that of his plays and Elizabethan poetry in general, is drawn chiefly from nature and everyday life, from business and law and the fine arts. A sonnet may work out a single metaphor (from business in 4, the seasons in 5, the sun in 7, music in 8), or, sometimes, may use a separate metaphor in each quatrain (as in 73 decay is treated in terms of summer and winter, day and night, fire and ashes), or (as in 1 and 19) may employ a new image in almost every line. A number of sonnets elaborate one metaphor – such as the art of the painter in 24 – with the most finespun ingenuity. This control of images, like that of the divisions of progressive argument with which it is bound up, is seldom relaxed or disrupted even in what appear to be the most deeply disturbed utterances. We are not surprised when, say, the serene exaltation of "Shall I compare thee to a summer's day?" (18) receives logical development; but 147, a violent revulsion from sensual love for the dark lady, is a no less ordered exposition of a ravaging fever incurable by reason.

The structure and texture of the sonnets combine a disciplined, orthodox formalism with the passionate ratiocination that we associate with the "metaphysical" poets – a strain that was emerging in the early 1590's, notably in Donne and Chapman. On the one hand, Shakespeare's style and rhythm, "the proud full sail of his great verse" (to quote his phrase about the rival poet), are mainly in the grand manner and have a smooth Italianate amplitude and flow, the rhetorical rotundity that we find in the earlier plays. One element in that effect is the abundant but discriminating use of alliteration and assonance – "the sessions of sweet silent thought" and "the surly sullen bell," to cite two simple examples. On the other hand, Shakespeare's diction (often monosyllabic) and images can be colloquial and homely, even when his argumentative conceits are most intricate – and to say that is to recall Coleridge's comment on Donne's and other old poets' expressing fantastic ideas in pure English. But, though active cerebration is always going on (and, like Donne's, does not always make poetry), the results are seldom intel-

lectualized through recondite allusion; annotation of the
sonnets requires the explaining, not of erudition, but of
obsolete words and idioms or complex density of thought.
And, while Donne's forceful language does its work in its
local context but carries little or no aura of suggestion,
Shakespeare's sets up rich reverberations – as lines quoted
in these pages remind us.

The characters and situations of Shakespeare's sonnets,
in diverging widely from the restricted Petrarchan tradi-
tion, freed him from many stereotyped themes, attitudes,
and images (sonnet 130 satirizes the conventional cata-
logue of feminine beauties). That is not to say that those
themes and attitudes – of which the most central was of
course the persuasive adoration of a reluctant or disdainful
mistress – did not evoke many fine sonnets from other
Elizabethan poets. Moreover, Shakespeare's young man,
like a Petrarchan mistress, is more loved than loving, and
ten dozen sonnets in praise of him and friendship can,
with all their fertile and graceful invention, fall at times
into a semi-Petrarchan monotony. Since modern readers
are unused to such ardor in masculine friendship and are
likely to leap at the notion of homosexuality (a notion
sufficiently refuted by the sonnets themselves), we may
remember that such an ideal – often exalted above the love
of women – could exist in real life, from Montaigne to Sir
Thomas Browne, and was conspicuous in Renaissance
literature (*Euphues*, Sidney's *Arcadia*, the fourth book of
The Faerie Queene, some of Shakespeare's plays), whether
on the merely human level or linked with cosmic concord.
The poet's young friend, though alive, familiarly known,
and sometimes charged with vices, becomes a kind of
equivalent of Donne's Elizabeth Drury, a symbol of living
perfection. It may be further remarked that one often
could not say, and does not need to ask, whether an indi-
vidual sonnet is concerned with love for a man or a woman;
one supreme example is "Let me not to the marriage of
true minds / Admit impediments" (116).

Indeed the "story" has value only in the poet's distilla-
tion of universal emotions and values. (The few indecent
sonnets, by the way, may be regretted, not because ob-
scenity cannot be functional, as it often is in the plays, but
because here the tone is brittle and jarring.) Most of the
great sonnets are at once self-sufficient units and notes in a
complex symphony. While the eternizing power of poetry
is an especially Renaissance theme, the modern reader,
even if he does not recall the proud claims of Ovid and
Horace, must be stirred by the forward-looking

> Not marble nor the gilded monuments
> Of princes shall outlive this pow'rful rime,

or by the backward-looking

> When in the chronicle of wasted time
> I see descriptions of the fairest wights,
> And beauty making beautiful old rime
> In praise of ladies dead and lovely knights....

But such passages are more than themselves; they are
partial expressions of the pervasive, all-embracing theme
of "Devouring Time" – a theme which inspired much of
the greatest poetry and prose of the English Renaissance.
Even writers, from Spenser and Raleigh to Browne and
Taylor, whose most earnest vision was fixed on heaven,
were poignantly conscious of the much-loved earth and
time and mutability. Shakespeare's voice – heard also
through Hamlet in the graveyard and elsewhere – is in the
sonnets mainly the outcry of the natural man against the
decay and extinction of beauty and vitality and love:

> Since brass, nor stone, nor earth, nor boundless sea,
> But sad mortality o'ersways their power,
> How with this rage shall beauty hold a plea,
> Whose action is no stronger than a flower?

Moments of unclouded happiness are moments only. The
objects of love – like the lover – are subject to time, from
"the darling buds of May" to "precious friends hid in

death's dateless night." The young friend, in his spring-time of life and pleasure, awakens thoughts of the poet's autumnal age, of leafless boughs, "Bare ruined choirs where late the sweet birds sang." Yet perhaps the greatest of all the sonnets is a defiant affirmation, the affirmation of a man who has no Platonic supports but only his human hold on the particular:

> Love's not Time's fool, though rosy lips and cheeks
> Within his bending sickle's compass come.

But the man sustained by love is still, like all human creatures, subject not only to destructive time but to in-ward evil. The main contrast in the sonnets, C. S. Lewis remarks, "is between the two loves, that 'of comfort' and that 'of despair'" (Sonnet 144). No conception was more deeply rooted in the Renaissance mind than the unceasing conflict in man between the bestial and the angelic ele-ments in his nature; and, of course, the finer the individual nature the more agonizing the conflict. What was said a while ago about the voice of "the natural man" in Shake-speare's sonnets must be qualified. It seems nowadays to be agreed that Shakespeare the dramatist shared the religi-ous beliefs of his fellow citizens, however far his imagina-tion might transcend popular orthodoxy; the appeals in the greater plays to Christian faith and Christian values are too numerous and too significant to be brushed off. If Elizabethan sonnets, like plays, were an essentially secular and naturalistic genre, none the less religion was too much an enveloping fact of life to be kept out. One incidental and unexpected – and, if not quite certain, strongly probable – reference at the end of Shakespeare's 110th sonnet ranks the poet's love for the young man next to the Christian heaven. But there are clearer and more important things.

In *Astrophel and Stella* Sidney had felt acute conflict be-tween the claims of illicit but ennobling love and the claims of Christian virtue, and the last group of Shake-speare's sonnets depict an illicit, intense, and far from ennobling passion for an unworthy woman. If the praises given to her charms are mostly conventional, the savage denunciations of her falsity go well beyond the considerable license permitted to sonneteers. While both attraction and repulsion are commonly painted in naturalistic terms, there are some appeals to the moral and the religious conscience. The most often-quoted testimony is "Th' expense of spirit in a waste of shame" (129), which is at once a naturalistic and rational and impassioned analysis of "lust in action"; and the sensual lover's "heaven" and "hell" are grimly ironic reminders of their religious counterparts. The religious consciousness is present likewise in 142, 144, and above all in 146 ("Poor soul, the center of my sinful earth"), a Shakespearean parallel to that detached sonnet of Sidney's, "Leave me, O love which reachest but to dust"; both combine the despair and the comfort of *contemptus mundi*. These sonnets, few in relation to the rest, still add a major dimension to the world of experience created in the series (as, to recall a very different context, a few lines add a similar dimension to the fleshly Wife of Bath). Shakespeare's world is composed of universal elements, beauty and decay, time and death, permanence and flux, truth and falsehood, and love in all its forms, from lust to "charity"; and the changes are rung on these timeless themes by an artist of supreme sensitivity to feeling and thought and word and rhythm.

Harvard University   DOUGLAS BUSH

NOTE ON THE TEXT

The only authority for the text of the sonnets other than 138 and 144, versions of which appeared in *The Passionate Pilgrim* (1599), is the quarto volume issued by Thomas Thorpe in 1609. Although this volume contains, in addition to the 154 sonnets, a poem of doubtful authenticity (*A Lover's Complaint*. "By William Shakespeare"), and although it is unlikely that it was printed from a manuscript in the author's own hand and certain that it was not proofread by him, it provides nevertheless a text which seems reliable in the main. A rearrangement of the sonnets pirated from Thorpe's quarto by John Benson in 1640 lacks independent authority. The present edition follows the text of the quarto of 1609 and retains its order of the sonnets. The following list of emendations is complete except for corrections of obvious misprints; the adopted reading is given in italics followed by the quarto reading in roman: 12:4 *all* or 13:7 *Yourself* You selfe 25:9 *fight* worth 26:12 *thy* their 27:10 *thy* their 28:14 *strength* length 31:8 *thee* there 34:12 *cross* losse 35:8 *thy . . . thy* their . . . their 37:7 *thy* their 39:12 *doth* dost 41:8 *she* he 43:11 *thy* their 45:12 *thy* their 46:3, 8, 13, 14 *thy* their 47:11 *not* nor 50:6 *dully* duly 51:11 *weigh* naigh 55:1 *monuments* monument 56:13 *Or* As 65:12 *of* or 69:3 *due* end 69:5 *Thy* Their 70:1 *art* are 70:6 *Thy* Their 74:12 *remembered* remembred 76:7 *tell* fel 77:10 *blanks* blacks 99:9 *One* Our 102:8 *her* his 112:14 *are* y'are 113:6 *latch* lack 113:14 *mine eye* mine 127:9 *brows* eyes 128:11 *thy* their 129:11 *proved, a* proud and 132:2 *torments* torment 132:6 *of the* of th' 132:9 *mourning* morning 144:6 *side* sight 146:2 *Fooled by* My sinfull earth 153:14 *eyes* eye. The spelling and punctuation have been modernized as in the other volumes of the present series. The glossarial notes, supplied by the general editor, are greatly indebted to the *New Variorum Edition* by Hyder Rollins (2 vols, 1944), a superb example of modern scholarship.

SHAKESPEARE'S
SONNETS

TO THE ONLY BEGETTER OF
THESE ENSUING SONNETS
MR. W. H. ALL HAPPINESS
AND THAT ETERNITY
PROMISED
BY
OUR EVER-LIVING POET
WISHETH
THE WELL-WISHING
ADVENTURER IN
SETTING
FORTH
T.T.

1

From fairest creatures we desire increase,
That thereby beauty's rose might never die,
But as the riper should by time decease,
His tender heir might bear his memory;   4
But thou, contracted to thine own bright eyes,
Feed'st thy light's flame with self-substantial fuel,
Making a famine where abundance lies,
Thyself thy foe, to thy sweet self too cruel.   8
Thou that art now the world's fresh ornament
And only herald to the gaudy spring,
Within thine own bud buriest thy content
And, tender churl, mak'st waste in niggarding.   12
    Pity the world, or else this glutton be,
      To eat the world's due, by the grave and thee.

2 *rose* (capitalized and italicized in Q)   5 *contracted* betrothed   6 *self-substantial* of your own substance   10 *only* principal   11 *thy content* what you contain (i.e. potentiality for parenthood; with play on 'self-satisfaction'?)   12 *niggarding* hoarding   14 *by . . . thee* i.e. by wilfully dying without issue

2

When forty winters shall besiege thy brow
And dig deep trenches in thy beauty's field,
Thy youth's proud livery, so gazed on now,
4   Will be a tottered weed of small worth held:
Then being asked where all thy beauty lies,
Where all the treasure of thy lusty days,
To say within thine own deep-sunken eyes
8   Were an all-eating shame and thriftless praise.
How much more praise deserved thy beauty's use
If thou couldst answer, 'This fair child of mine
Shall sum my count and make my old excuse,'
12   Proving his beauty by succession thine.
    This were to be new made when thou art old
    And see thy blood warm when thou feel'st it cold.

2 *trenches* furrows, wrinkles   3 *livery* marks, fittings   4 *tottered weed* tattered garment   8 *thriftless* unprofitable   9 *use* investment   11 *sum . . . excuse* i.e. even my account and make amends for growing old

3

Look in thy glass, and tell the face thou viewest
Now is the time that face should form another,
Whose fresh repair if now thou not renewest,
Thou dost beguile the world, unbless some mother.   4
For where is she so fair whose uneared womb
Disdains the tillage of thy husbandry?
Or who is he so fond will be the tomb
Of his self-love, to stop posterity?   8
Thou art thy mother's glass, and she in thee
Calls back the lovely April of her prime;
So thou through windows of thine age shalt see,
Despite of wrinkles, this thy golden time.   12
    But if thou live rememb'red not to be,
    Die single, and thine image dies with thee.

3 *fresh repair* youthful state   4 *unbless some mother* fail to bless some woman with motherhood   5 *uneared* untilled   7 *fond* foolish; *tomb* monument   8 *to stop posterity* thus bringing an end to his line   11 *windows . . . age* apertures in the enclosure of old age   13 *rememb'red . . . be* to be forgotten

4

Unthrifty loveliness, why dost thou spend
Upon thyself thy beauty's legacy?
Nature's bequest gives nothing but doth lend,
4   And, being frank, she lends to those are free.
Then, beauteous niggard, why dost thou abuse
The bounteous largess given thee to give?
Profitless usurer, why dost thou use
8   So great a sum of sums, yet canst not live?
For, having traffic with thyself alone,
Thou of thyself thy sweet self dost deceive:
Then how, when Nature calls thee to be gone,
12   What acceptable audit canst thou leave?
    Thy unused beauty must be tombed with thee,
    Which, usèd, lives th' executor to be.

2 *beauty's legacy* inheritance of beauty   3–4 *Nature's . . . free* (cf. parable of the talents, Matthew xxv, 14–30, and *Measure for Measure*, I, i, 36–40) 4 *frank* generous; *free* generous 5 *niggard* miser 7 *use* invest 8 *live* (1) make a living, (2) survive through posterity 9 *traffic* commerce 10 *deceive* cheat 14 *lives* i.e. in the person of a son

5

Those hours that with gentle work did frame
The lovely gaze where every eye doth dwell
Will play the tyrants to the very same
And that unfair which fairly doth excel;   4
For never-resting time leads summer on
To hideous winter and confounds him there,
Sap checked with frost and lusty leaves quite gone,
Beauty o'ersnowed and bareness everywhere.   8
Then, were not summer's distillation left
A liquid prisoner pent in walls of glass,
Beauty's effect with beauty were bereft,
Nor it nor no remembrance what it was: 12
    But flowers distilled, though they with winter meet,
    Leese but their show; their substance still lives sweet.

2 *gaze* object of gazes, cynosure 4 *unfair* deface; *fairly* in beauty 6 *confounds* destroys 9 *summer's distillation* essence of flowers, perfumes 11 *were bereft* would be taken away 12 *Nor it* (leaving behind) neither itself 14 *Leese* lose

6

Then let not winter's ragged hand deface
In thee thy summer ere thou be distilled:
Make sweet some vial; treasure thou some place
4   With beauty's treasure ere it be self-killed.
That use is not forbidden usury
Which happies those that pay the willing loan;
That's for thyself to breed another thee,
8   Or ten times happier be it ten for one.
Ten times thyself were happier than thou art,
If ten of thine ten times refigured thee:
Then what could death do if thou shouldst depart,
12   Leaving thee living in posterity?
    Be not self-willed, for thou art much too fair
    To be death's conquest and make worms thine heir.

1 *ragged* rough 3 *treasure* enrich 5 *forbidden usury* (lending money at interest – 'use' – had formerly been illegal) 6 *happies . . . loan* makes happy those who willingly pay for the loan 9 *happier* better, luckier 10 *refigured* duplicated

7

Lo, in the orient when the gracious light
Lifts up his burning head, each under eye
Doth homage to his new-appearing sight,
Serving with looks his sacred majesty;   4
And having climbed the steep-up heavenly hill,
Resembling strong youth in his middle age,
Yet mortal looks adore his beauty still,
Attending on his golden pilgrimage;   8
But when from highmost pitch, with weary car,
Like feeble age he reeleth from the day,
The eyes, fore duteous, now converted are
From his low tract and look another way: 12
    So thou, thyself outgoing in thy noon,
    Unlooked on diest unless thou get a son.

1 *orient* east; *light* sun   2 *each under eye* each eye on earth below   5 *steep-up* precipitous   9 *highmost pitch* apex; *car* Phoebus' chariot   11 *fore* before; *converted* turned away   12 *tract* course   13 *outgoing . . . noon* i.e. passing your prime

8

Music to hear, why hear'st thou music sadly?
Sweets with sweets war not, joy delights in joy:
Why lov'st thou that which thou receiv'st not gladly,
4   Or else receiv'st with pleasure thine annoy?
If the true concord of well-tunèd sounds,
By unions married, do offend thine ear,
They do but sweetly chide thee, who confounds
8   In singleness the parts that thou shouldst bear.
Mark how one string, sweet husband to another,
Strikes each in each by mutual ordering;
Resembling sire and child and happy mother,
12   Who, all in one, one pleasing note do sing;
     Whose speechless song, being many, seeming one,
     Sings this to thee, 'Thou single wilt prove none.'

1 *Music to hear* you whom it is music to hear (a vocative); *sadly* soberly, without joy   3–4 *Why . . . annoy* i.e. you must either love what gives you no pleasure, or else take pleasure in what annoys you   7–8 *confounds . . . bear* i.e. spoils the harmony (of marriage) by performing singly instead of in concert   14 *none* no one, nothing

9

Is it for fear to wet a widow's eye
That thou consum'st thyself in single life?
Ah, if thou issueless shalt hap to die,
The world will wail thee like a makeless wife;   4
The world will be thy widow, and still weep
That thou no form of thee hast left behind,
When every private widow well may keep,
By children's eyes, her husband's shape in mind.   8
Look what an unthrift in the world doth spend
Shifts but his place, for still the world enjoys it;
But beauty's waste hath in the world an end,
And, kept unused, the user so destroys it: 12
    No love toward others in that bosom sits
    That on himself such murd'rous shame commits.

3 *issueless* childless **4** *makeless* mateless **7** *private* particular **9** *Look what* whatever; *unthrift* prodigal **10** *his* its **14** *murd'rous shame* shameful murder

IO

For shame, deny that thou bear'st love to any
Who for thyself art so unprovident:
Grant, if thou wilt, thou art beloved of many,
But that thou none lov'st is most evident;
For thou art so possessed with murd'rous hate
That 'gainst thyself thou stick'st not to conspire,
Seeking that beauteous roof to ruinate
Which to repair should be thy chief desire.
O, change thy thought, that I may change my mind;
Shall hate be fairer lodged than gentle love?
Be as thy presence is, gracious and kind,
Or to thyself at least kind-hearted prove:
　　Make thee another self for love of me,
　　That beauty still may live in thine or thee.

6 *thou stick'st* you scruple　7 *roof* structure (your person); *ruinate* ruin
9 *change my mind* think otherwise　11 *presence* appearance　14 *still* always

II

As fast as thou shalt wane, so fast thou grow'st
In one of thine, from that which thou departest;
And that fresh blood which youngly thou bestow'st
Thou mayst call thine when thou from youth convertest.　　**4**
Herein lives wisdom, beauty, and increase;
Without this, folly, age, and cold decay.
If all were minded so, the times should cease,
And threescore year would make the world away.　　**8**
Let those whom Nature hath not made for store,
Harsh, featureless, and rude, barrenly perish:
Look whom she best endowed she gave the more,
Which bounteous gift thou shouldst in bounty cherish.　　**12**
　　She carved thee for her seal, and meant thereby
　　Thou shouldst print more, not let that copy die.

1–2 *thou grow'st . . . departest* i.e. you become, in one of your children, what you cease to be in yourself　3 *youngly* in youth　4 *thou . . . convertest* you . . . turn away　7 *times* generations of man　9 *store* replenishment　10 *featureless* ill-featured　11 *Look whom* whomever　13 *seal* stamp from which impressions are made

12

When I do count the clock that tells the time
And see the brave day sunk in hideous night,
When I behold the violet past prime
4   And sable curls all silvered o'er with white,
When lofty trees I see barren of leaves,
Which erst from heat did canopy the herd,
And summer's green all girded up in sheaves
8   Borne on the bier with white and bristly beard;
Then of thy beauty do I question make
That thou among the wastes of time must go,
Since sweets and beauties do themselves forsake
12   And die as fast as they see others grow;
        And nothing 'gainst Time's scythe can make defense
        Save breed, to brave him when he takes thee hence.

2 *brave* splendid   4 *sable* black   6 *erst* formerly   7 *summer's green* i.e.
wheat   8 *bier* i.e. the harvest cart   9 *question make* speculate   14 *breed*
offspring; *brave* defv

13

O, that you were yourself, but, love, you are
No longer yours than you yourself here live:
Against this coming end you should prepare,
And your sweet semblance to some other give.   4
So should that beauty which you hold in lease
Find no determination; then you were
Yourself again after yourself's decease
When your sweet issue your sweet form should bear.   8
Who lets so fair a house fall to decay,
Which husbandry in honor might uphold
Against the stormy gusts of winter's day
And barren rage of death's eternal cold?   12
    O, none but unthrifts! Dear my love, you know
    You had a father – let your son say so.

1 *O . . . yourself* i.e. O, that your eternal self and present self were one
5 *in lease* i.e. for a term   6 *determination* end   8 *issue* offspring   10 *husbandry* thrifty management (with pun on 'marriage')   13 *unthrifts* prodigals

14

Not from the stars do I my judgment pluck,
And yet methinks I have astronomy;
But not to tell of good or evil luck,
4   Of plagues, of dearths, or seasons' quality;
Nor can I fortune to brief minutes tell,
Pointing to each his thunder, rain, and wind,
Or say with princes if it shall go well
8   By oft predict that I in heaven find;
But from thine eyes my knowledge I derive,
And, constant stars, in them I read such art
As truth and beauty shall together thrive
12   If from thyself to store thou wouldst convert:
    Or else of thee this I prognosticate,
    Thy end is truth's and beauty's doom and date.

---

1 *judgment* opinion; *pluck* derive   2 *astronomy* astrology   5 *fortune . . . tell*
i.e. foretell the events of every moment   6 *Pointing* appointing; *his* its   8
oft predict that frequent prediction of what   10 *read such art* gather such
lore   11 *As* as that   12 *store* replenishment; *convert* turn   14 *doom and
date* prescribed end

15

When I consider everything that grows
Holds in perfection but a little moment,
That this huge stage presenteth nought but shows
Whereon the stars in secret influence comment;   4
When I perceive that men as plants increase,
Cheerèd and checked even by the selfsame sky,
Vaunt in their youthful sap, at height decrease,
And wear their brave state out of memory: 8
Then the conceit of this inconstant stay
Sets you most rich in youth before my sight,
Where wasteful Time debateth with Decay
To change your day of youth to sullied night;   12
    And, all in war with Tɪme for love of you,
    As he takes from you, I ingraft you new.

---

3 *stage* the world   **4** *in secret . . . comment* i.e. provide a silent commentary by influencing the action   **6** *Cheerèd and checked* (1) applauded and hissed, (2) nourished and starved   **7** *Vaunt* boast; *sap* i.e. vigor   **8** *brave* splendid; *out of memory* i.e. until forgotten   **9** *conceit* idea; *stay* duration   **11** *wasteful* destructive; *debateth* joins forces, fights   **14** *ingraft* graft, infuse new life into (with poetry)

16

But wherefore do not you a mightier way
Make war upon this bloody tyrant, Time?
And fortify yourself in your decay
4   With means more blessèd than my barren rime?
Now stand you on the top of happy hours,
And many maiden gardens, yet unset,
With virtuous wish would bear your living flowers,
8   Much liker than your painted counterfeit:
So should the lines of life that life repair
Which this time's pencil or my pupil pen,
Neither in inward worth nor outward fair
12 Can make you live yourself in eyes of men.
　　To give away yourself keeps yourself still,
　　And you must live, drawn by your own sweet skill.

5 *on the top* at the peak　6 *unset* unplanted　7 *wish* i.e. willingness　8 *counterfeit* portrait　9 *lines of life* living lineaments (of children)　10 *this time's pencil* contemporary portraiture; *pupil* inexpert　11 *fair* beauty　13 *give away yourself* i.e. transfer yourself into children

17

Who will believe my verse in time to come
If it were filled with your most high deserts?
Though yet, heaven knows, it is but as a tomb
Which hides your life and shows not half your parts.   4
If I could write the beauty of your eyes
And in fresh numbers number all your graces,
The age to come would say, 'This poet lies –
Such heavenly touches ne'er touched earthly faces.'   8
So should my papers, yellowed with their age,
Be scorned, like old men of less truth than tongue,
And your true rights be termed a poet's rage
And stretchèd metre of an antique song.   12
    But were some child of yours alive that time,
    You should live twice – in it and in my rime.

2 *deserts* merits   4 *parts* qualities   6 *numbers* verses   8 *touches* strokes
of artistry   11 *true rights* due praise   12 *stretchèd metre* poetic hyperbole
13 *that time* in that future time

18

Shall I compare thee to a summer's day?
Thou art more lovely and more temperate.
Rough winds do shake the darling buds of May,
4   And summer's lease hath all too short a date.
Sometime too hot the eye of heaven shines,
And often is his gold complexion dimmed;
And every fair from fair sometime declines,
8   By chance, or nature's changing course, untrimmed:
But thy eternal summer shall not fade
Nor lose possession of that fair thou ow'st,
Nor shall Death brag thou wand'rest in his shade
12   When in eternal lines to time thou grow'st
            So long as men can breathe or eyes can see,
            So long lives this, and this gives life to thee.

4 *lease* allotted time; *date* duration   5 *eye* sun   6 *dimmed* clouded over
7 *fair from fair* beautiful thing from beauty   8 *untrimmed* stripped of
adornment   10 *thou ow'st* you own   11 *shade* i.e. oblivion   12 *lines* poetry;
thou grow'st you are grafted

19

Devouring Time, blunt thou the lion's paws,
And make the earth devour her own sweet brood;
Pluck the keen teeth from the fierce tiger's jaws,
And burn the long-lived phoenix in her blood;   4
Make glad and sorry seasons as thou fleet'st,
And do whate'er thou wilt, swift-footed Time,
To the wide world and all her fading sweets,
But I forbid thee one most heinous crime: 8
O, carve not with thy hours my love's fair brow,
Nor draw no lines there with thine antique pen;
Him in thy course untainted do allow
For beauty's pattern to succeeding men.   12
 Yet do thy worst, old Time: despite thy wrong,
 My love shall in my verse ever live young.

---

2 *brood* i.e. the children of earth **4** *phoenix* a legendary bird which lives
for hundreds of years and then propagates itself from its own ashes (symbol
of immortality); *in her blood* alive **10** *antique* (1) antic, capricious, (2) old
11 *untainted* unspoiled

20

A woman's face, with Nature's own hand painted,
Hast thou, the master-mistress of my passion;
A woman's gentle heart, but not acquainted
4   With shifting change, as is false women's fashion;
An eye more bright than theirs, less false in rolling,
Gilding the object whereupon it gazeth;
A man in hue all hues in his controlling,
8   Which steals men's eyes and women's souls amazeth.
And for a woman wert thou first created,
Till Nature as she wrought thee fell a-doting,
And by addition me of thee defeated
12   By adding one thing to my purpose nothing.
    But since she pricked thee out for women's pleasure,
    Mine be thy love, and thy love's use their treasure.

1 *with . . . hand* i.e. naturally, without cosmetics 2 *master-mistress* master and mistress; *passion* love 5 *rolling* i.e. passing from one to another 6 *Gilding* brightening (as do the rays of the sun) 7 *A man . . . controlling* i.e. a man in complexion with all complexions – 'humors' – under his control (the line may be corrupt or, as glossed thus, may contrast male constancy with feminine inconstancy); *hues* (capitalized and italicized in Q) 11 *defeated* cheated, deprived 12 *one thing* i.e. a penis

21

So is it not with me as with that Muse
Stirred by a painted beauty to his verse,
Who heaven itself for ornament doth use
And every fair with his fair doth rehearse;   4
Making a couplement of proud compare
With sun and moon, with earth and sea's rich gems,
With April's first-born flowers, and all things rare
That heaven's air in this huge rondure hems.   8
O let me, true in love, but truly write,
And then believe me, my love is as fair
As any mother's child, though not so bright
As those gold candles fixed in heaven's air: 12
    Let them say more that like of hearsay well;
    I will not praise that purpose not to sell.

---

1 *Muse* poet **2** *Stirred . . . beauty* inspired by artificial beauty **4** *every . . rehearse* i.e. mentions everything beautiful in relation to his mistress **5** *couplement* combination; *compare* comparison **8** *rondure* sphere; *hems* encircles **12** *gold candles* i.e. stars **13** *that . . . well* i.e. that are fond of large and specious comparisons **14** *that* who, i.e. since I am not a huckster

22

My glass shall not persuade me I am old
So long as youth and thou are of one date;
But when in thee time's furrows I behold,
4 Then look I death my days should expiate.
For all that beauty that doth cover thee
Is but the seemly raiment of my heart,
Which in thy breast doth live, as thine in me:
8 How can I then be elder than thou art?
O therefore, love, be of thyself so wary
As I, not for myself, but for thee will,
Bearing thy heart, which I will keep so chary
12 As tender nurse her babe from faring ill.
    Presume not on thy heart when mine is slain;
    Thou gav'st me thine not to give back again.

2 *of one date* of an age; i.e. so long as you are young   4 *expiate* wind up
5–8 *For . . . art* i.e. the friend's beautiful body encloses the poet's heart,
and this transfer of hearts makes friend and poet of one age   11 *chary*
carefully   13 *Presume not on* do not expect to regain

23

As an unperfect actor on the stage,
Who with his fear is put besides his part,
Or some fierce thing replete with too much rage,
Whose strength's abundance weakens his own heart; 4
So I, for fear of trust, forget to say
The perfect ceremony of love's rite,
And in mine own love's strength seem to decay,
O'ercharged with burden of mine own love's might. 8
O, let my books be then the eloquence
And dumb presagers of my speaking breast,
Who plead for love, and look for recompense,
More than that tongue that more hath more expressed. 12
    O, learn to read what silent love hath writ:
    To hear with eyes belongs to love's fine wit.

1 *unperfect actor* i.e. imperfect in his craft or in his part 2 *besides* out of
4 *heart* i.e. capacity for performance 5 *for . . . trust* in self-distrust 5–6
forget . . . rite i.e. am not word-perfect in love's ritual 7 *decay* i.e. falter
10 *dumb presagers* silent messengers 12 *more expressed* more often ex-
pressed 14 *wit* intelligence

24

Mine eye hath played the painter and hath stelled
Thy beauty's form in table of my heart;
My body is the frame wherein 'tis held,
4   And perspective it is best painter's art.
For through the painter must you see his skill
To find where your true image pictured lies,
Which in my bosom's shop is hanging still,
8   That hath his windows glazèd with thine eyes.
Now see what good turns eyes for eyes have done:
Mine eyes have drawn thy shape, and thine for me
Are windows to my breast, wherethrough the sun
12   Delights to peep, to gaze therein on thee.
    Yet eyes this cunning want to grace their art;
    They draw but what they see, know not the heart.

---

1 *stelled* portrayed   2 *table* tablet (?), picture (?)   4 *perspective it is* i.e. given perspective, which is (?)   8 *his* its; *glazèd* paned   13 *cunning* skill; *want* lack; *grace* enhance

25

Let those who are in favor with their stars
Of public honor and proud titles boast,
Whilst I, whom fortune of such triumph bars,
Unlooked for joy in that I honor most.   4
Great princes' favorites their fair leaves spread
But as the marigold at the sun's eye;
And in themselves their pride lies burièd,
For at a frown they in their glory die.   8
The painful warrior famousèd for fight,
After a thousand victories once foiled,
Is from the book of honor rasèd quite,
And all the rest forgot for which he toiled.   12
    Then happy I, that love and am beloved
    Where I may not remove nor be removed.

---

1 *who . . . stars* i.e. whose stars are propitious   4 *Unlooked for* unexpectedly;
that what   6 *But* only   7 *lies burièd* i.e. is already in its grave   9 *painful*
striving; *fight* (an emendation for 'worth'; some editors retain 'worth' and
emend *quite* in l. 11 to 'forth')   11 *rasèd* erased

26

Lord of my love, to whom in vassalage
Thy merit hath my duty strongly knit,
To thee I send this written ambassage
4 To witness duty, not to show my wit;
Duty so great, which wit so poor as mine
May make seem bare, in wanting words to show it,
But that I hope some good conceit of thine
8 In thy soul's thought, all naked, will bestow it;
Till whatsoever star that guides my moving
Points on me graciously with fair aspect,
And puts apparel on my tottered loving
12 To show me worthy of thy sweet respect:
    Then may I dare to boast how I do love thee;
    Till then not show my head where thou mayst prove me.

3 *ambassage* overture, message (probably the present sonnet) 4 *wit* poetic powers 7 *conceit* conception 8 *all . . . bestow it* i.e. will give it lodging despite its nakedness 9 *moving* i.e. life and actions 10 *aspect* influence (astrological term) 11 *tottered* tattered 14 *prove* test

27

Weary with toil, I haste me to my bed,
The dear repose for limbs with travel tired,
But then begins a journey in my head
To work my mind when body's work's expired;   4
For then my thoughts, from far where I abide,
Intend a zealous pilgrimage to thee,
And keep my drooping eyelids open wide,
Looking on darkness which the blind do see;   8
Save that my soul's imaginary sight
Presents thy shadow to my sightless view,
Which, like a jewel hung in ghastly night,
Makes black night beauteous and her old face new.   12
    Lo, thus, by day my limbs, by night my mind,
    For thee and for myself no quiet find.

2 *travel* (1) journeying, (2) travail   4 *To work* to set to work   6 *pilgrimage*
journey of devotion   8 *which* such as   9 *imaginary* imagining   10 *shadow*
image

28

How can I then return in happy plight
That am debarred the benefit of rest,
When day's oppression is not eased by night,
4 But day by night and night by day oppressed,
And each, though enemies to either's reign,
Do in consent shake hands to torture me,
The one by toil, the other to complain
8 How far I toil, still farther off from thee?
I tell the day, to please him, thou art bright
And dost him grace when clouds do blot the heaven;
So flatter I the swart-complexioned night,
12 When sparkling stars twire not, thou gild'st the even.
But day doth daily draw my sorrows longer,
And night doth nightly make grief's strength seem stronger.

6 *shake hands* unite   7 *the other to complain* i.e. the night making me
complain   9 *I tell . . . bright* i.e. I please the day by telling him you are
bright   10 *And . . . heaven* and can shine in his place when it is cloudy   11
swart dark   12 *twire* peek; *thou . . . even* you make the evening bright

29

When, in disgrace with Fortune and men's eyes,
I all alone beweep my outcast state,
And trouble deaf heaven with my bootless cries,
And look upon myself and curse my fate,   4
Wishing me like to one more rich in hope,
Featured like him, like him with friends possessed,
Desiring this man's art, and that man's scope,
With what I most enjoy contented least;   8
Yet in these thoughts myself almost despising,
Haply I think on thee, and then my state,
Like to the lark at break of day arising
From sullen earth, sings hymns at heaven's gate;   12
    For thy sweet love rememb'red such wealth brings
    That then I scorn to change my state with kings.

1 *disgrace* disfavor; *eyes* regard   3 *bootless* useless   6 *like him, like him* i.e. like another, like still another   7 *art* literary skill; *scope* intellectual power   10 *Haply* perchance; *state* i.e. mood, state of mind   12 *sullen* gloomy   14 *state* lot

30

When to the sessions of sweet silent thought
I summon up remembrance of things past,
I sigh the lack of many a thing I sought,
4   And with old woes new wail my dear time's waste:
Then can I drown an eye, unused to flow,
For precious friends hid in death's dateless night,
And weep afresh love's long since cancelled woe,
8   And moan th' expense of many a vanished sight.
Then can I grieve at grievances foregone,
And heavily from woe to woe tell o'er
The sad account of fore-bemoanèd moan,
12   Which I new pay as if not paid before.
     But if the while I think on thee, dear friend,
     All losses are restored and sorrows end.

1 *sessions* sittings, as of a court   3 *sigh* lament   4 *new wail* newly bewail;
dear time's waste time's destruction of precious things (?), the wasteful
passing of precious time (?)   6 *dateless* endless   7 *cancelled* fully paid   8
expense loss   9 *foregone* former   10 *tell* count

31

Thy bosom is endearèd with all hearts
Which I by lacking have supposèd dead;
And there reigns love, and all love's loving parts,
And all those friends which I thought burièd.   4
How many a holy and obsequious tear
Hath dear religious love stol'n from mine eye,
As interest of the dead, which now appear
But things removed that hidden in thee lie!   8
Thou art the grave were buried love doth live,
Hung with the trophies of my lovers gone,
Who all their parts of me to thee did give;
That due of many now is thine alone.   12
    Their images I loved I view in thee,
    And thou, all they, hast all the all of me.

---

1 *endearèd* enriched 5 *obsequious* mourning 6 *religious* venerating
7 *interest* rightful due; *which* who 8 *removed* absent 10 *trophies* memo-
rials; *lovers* loved ones 11 *parts* shares 12 *That . . . many* what was due
to many 14 *all they* who are all of them combined

32

If thou survive my well-contented day
When that churl Death my bones with dust shall cover,
And shalt by fortune once more resurvey
4   These poor rude lines of thy deceasèd lover,
Compare them with the bett'ring of the time,
And though they be outstripped by every pen,
Reserve them for my love, not for their rime,
8   Exceeded by the height of happier men.
O, then vouchsafe me but this loving thought:
'Had my friend's Muse grown with this growing age,
A dearer birth than this his love had brought
12   To march in ranks of better equipage;
        But since he died, and poets better prove,
        Theirs for their style I'll read, his for his love.'

1 *my well-contented day* i.e. the ripe day of my death   5 *bett'ring* improved writing   7 *Reserve* preserve; *rime* poetic skill   8 *height* superiority; *happier* more gifted   11 *dearer* more precious   12 *of better equipage* more finely equipped

33

Full many a glorious morning have I seen
Flatter the mountain tops with sovereign eye,
Kissing with golden face the meadows green,
Gilding pale streams with heavenly alchemy;   4
Anon permit the basest clouds to ride
With ugly rack on his celestial face,
And from the forlorn world his visage hide,
Stealing unseen to west with this disgrace: 8
Even so my sun one early morn did shine
With all-triumphant splendor on my brow;
But, out alack, he was but one hour mine,
The region cloud hath masked him from me now.   12
    Yet him for this my love no whit disdaineth;
    Suns of the world may stain when heaven's sun staineth.

2 *Flatter . . . eye* i.e. honor with a royal glance of the sun   5 *Anon* soon;
basest darkest   6 *rack* cloud streamers   7 *forlorn* sadly forsaken   11 *out alack* alas   12 *region cloud* clouds of the upper air

34

Why didst thou promise such a beauteous day
And make me travel forth without my cloak,
To let base clouds o'ertake me in my way,
4   Hiding thy brav'ry in their rotten smoke?
'Tis not enough that through the cloud thou break
To dry the rain on my storm-beaten face,
For no man well of such a salve can speak
8   That heals the wound, and cures not the disgrace:
Nor can thy shame give physic to my grief;
Though thou repent, yet I have still the loss:
Th' offender's sorrow lends but weak relief
12   To him that bears the strong offense's cross.
    Ah, but those tears are pearl which thy love sheeds,
    And they are rich and ransom all ill deeds.

3 *base* dark   4 *brav'ry* splendor; *rotten smoke* unwholesome vapors
8 *disgrace* shame   9 *shame* regret; *physic* remedy   13 *sheeds* sheds   14
ransom atone for

35

No more be grieved at that which thou hast done:
Roses have thorns, and silver fountains mud;
Clouds and eclipses stain both moon and sun,
And loathsome canker lives in sweetest bud.   4
All men make faults, and even I in this,
Authorizing thy trespass with compare,
Myself corrupting, salving thy amiss,
Excusing thy sins more than thy sins are;   8
For to thy sensual fault I bring in sense
(Thy adverse party is thy advocate)
And 'gainst myself a lawful plea commence;
Such civil war is in my love and hate   12
    That I an accessary needs must be
    To that sweet thief which sourly robs from me.

---

3 *stain* darken 4 *canker* destroying worm 5 *make faults* are faulty
6 *Authorizing* justifying; *with compare* by comparison 7 *salving thy amiss*
palliating your offense 8 *Excusing . . . are* i.e. going further in excusing
your sins than you in sinning 9 *to . . . sense* i.e. to your physical fault I add
my intellectual fault (perhaps with a pun on 'incense') 13 *accessary*
fellow sinner

36

Let me confess that we two must be twain
Although our undivided loves are one:
So shall those blots that do with me remain,
4   Without thy help by me be borne alone.
In our two loves there is but one respect,
Though in our lives a separable spite,
Which though it alter not love's sole effect,
8   Yet doth it steal sweet hours from love's delight.
I may not evermore acknowledge thee,
Lest my bewailèd guilt should do thee shame;
Nor thou with public kindness honor me
12   Unless thou take that honor from thy name:
          But do not so; I love thee in such sort
          As, thou being mine, mine is thy good report.

3 *blots* defects   5 *but one respect* a singleness of attitude   6 *separable
spite* spiteful separation   7 *sole* singleness of   10 *bewailèd* lamented   14
report reputation

37

As a decrepit father takes delight
To see his active child do deeds of youth,
So I, made lame by Fortune's dearest spite,
Take all my comfort of thy worth and truth.   4
For whether beauty, birth, or wealth, or wit,
Or any of these all, or all, or more,
Intitled in thy parts do crownèd sit,
I make my love ingrafted to this store.   8
So then I am not lame, poor, nor despised
Whilst that this shadow doth such substance give
That I in thy abundance am sufficed
And by a part of all thy glory live.   12
    Look what is best, that best I wish in thee.
    This wish I have; then ten times happy me!

3 *made lame* i.e. handicapped (in a general sense); *dearest* most grievous
4 *of* in 5 *wit* intelligence 7 *Intitled . . . sit* sit enthroned among your
qualities 8 *ingrafted . . . store* i.e. fastened to and drawing upon this
abundance 10 *shadow* the idea; *substance* the actuality 13 *Look what*
whatever

38

How can my Muse want subject to invent
While thou dost breathe, that pour'st into my verse
Thine own sweet argument, too excellent
4 For every vulgar paper to rehearse?
O, give thyself the thanks if aught in me
Worthy perusal stand against thy sight,
For who's so dumb that cannot write to thee
8 When thou thyself dost give invention light?
Be thou the tenth Muse, ten times more in worth
Than those old nine which rimers invocate;
And he that calls on thee, let him bring forth
12 Eternal numbers to outlive long date.
 If my slight Muse do please these curious days,
 The pain be mine, but thine shall be the praise.

1 *want . . . invent* lack subject matter 3 *argument* theme 4 *vulgar paper* common composition 5 *in me* of mine 6 *stand . . . sight* meet your eye 8 *invention* power of creation 10 *invocate* invoke 12 *numbers* verses; *long* a distant 13 *curious* critical 14 *pain* painstaking

39

O, how thy worth with manners may I sing
When thou art all the better part of me?
What can mine own praise to mine own self bring,
And what is't but mine own when I praise thee?   4
Even for this let us divided live
And our dear love lose name of single one,
That by this separation I may give
That due to thee which thou deserv'st alone.   8
O absence, what a torment wouldst thou prove
Were it not thy sour leisure gave sweet leave
To entertain the time with thoughts of love,
Which time and thoughts so sweetly doth deceive,   12
    And that thou teachest how to make one twain
    By praising him here who doth hence remain!

1 *manners* modesty   5 *for* because of   6 *name* report   8 *That due* what is owing   11 *entertain* pass   12 *thoughts* melancholy; *deceive* beguile away   13 *And . . . twain* i.e. and were it not that you teach how to divide one into two

40

Take all my loves, my love, yea, take them all:
What hast thou then more than thou hadst before?
No love, my love, that thou mayst true love call;
4   All mine was thine before thou hadst this more.
Then, if for my love thou my love receivest,
I cannot blame thee for my love thou usest;
But yet be blamed if thou this self deceivest
8   By wilful taste of what thyself refusest.
I do forgive thy robb'ry, gentle thief,
Although thou steal thee all my poverty;
And yet love knows it is a greater grief
12   To bear love's wrong than hate's known injury.
      Lascivious grace, in whom all ill well shows,
      Kill me with spites; yet we must not be foes.

---

1 *Take . . . loves* (read in the context of later sonnets, the allusion seems to be to the poet's mistress whom the friend has taken) 6 *for* because; *thou usest* you enjoy 7 *this self* i.e. this one of your selves, the poet (often emended to 'thyself' without marked improvement of the sense) 8 *wilful taste of* i.e. capricious dalliance with (?); *thyself* i.e. your true self (?) 10 *my poverty* my little 12 *known* open, intended 13 *Lascivious grace* you who are gracious even in your amours

41

Those pretty wrongs that liberty commits
When I am sometime absent from thy heart,
Thy beauty and thy years full well befits,
For still temptation follows where thou art.   4
Gentle thou art, and therefore to be won;
Beauteous thou art, therefore to be assailed;
And when a woman woos, what woman's son
Will sourly leave her till she have prevailed?   8
Ay me, but yet thou mightst my seat forbear,
And chide thy beauty and thy straying youth,
Who lead thee in their riot even there
Where thou art forced to break a twofold truth: 12
 Hers, by thy beauty tempting her to thee,
 Thine, by thy beauty being false to me.

1 *pretty wrongs* peccadilloes; *liberty* license   3 *befits* makes inevitable
4 *still* always   9 *my seat forbear* forgo the place belonging to me   11 *Who*
which; *riot* revels

42

That thou hast her, it is not all my grief,
And yet it may be said I loved her dearly;
That she hath thee is of my wailing chief,
A loss in love that touches me more nearly.
Loving offenders, thus I will excuse ye:
Thou dost love her because thou know'st I love her,
And for my sake even so doth she abuse me,
Suff'ring my friend for my sake to approve her.
If I lose thee, my loss is my love's gain,
And losing her, my friend hath found that loss:
Both find each other, and I lose both twain,
And both for my sake lay on me this cross.
    But here's the joy: my friend and I are one;
    Sweet flattery! then she loves but me alone.

3 *of my wailing chief* my chief lament 7 *abuse* betray 8 *approve* prove,
try 9 *love's* mistress's 12 *cross* affliction

43

When most I wink, then do mine eyes best see,
For all the day they view things unrespected;
But when I sleep, in dreams they look on thee
And, darkly bright, are bright in dark directed.   4
Then thou, whose shadow shadows doth make bright,
How would thy shadow's form form happy show
To the clear day with thy much clearer light
When to unseeing eyes thy shade shines so!   8
How would, I say, mine eyes be blessèd made
By looking on thee in the living day,
When in dead night thy fair imperfect shade
Through heavy sleep on sightless eyes doth stay!   12
    All days are nights to see till I see thee,
    And nights bright days when dreams do show thee me.

1 *wink* shut my eyes in sleep   2 *unrespected* unnoticed   4 *darkly . . . directed* i.e. mysteriously lighted, see clearly in the dark   5 *shadow shadows* image darkness   6 *shadow's form* actual body   14 *show thee me* show you to me

44

If the dull substance of my flesh were thought,
Injurious distance should not stop my way;
For then, despite of space, I would be brought,
4 From limits far remote, where thou dost stay.
No matter then although my foot did stand
Upon the farthest earth removed from thee;
For nimble thought can jump both sea and land
8 As soon as think the place where he would be.
But, ah, thought kills me that I am not thought,
To leap large lengths of miles when thou art gone,
But that, so much of earth and water wrought,
12 I must attend time's leisure with my moan,
    Receiving naught by elements so slow
    But heavy tears, badges of either's woe.

1 *dull substance* i.e earth and water (dull as compared with the other
elements, fire and air) 2 *Injurious* spiteful 4 *limits* bounds; *where* to
where 6 *farthest earth* earth farthest 9 *ah, thought* ah, the thought 11
wrought fashioned 12 *attend* await 14 *either's woe* (i.e. the earth sup-
plies the weight, the water the moisture of the 'heavy tears')

45

The other two, slight air and purging fire,
Are both with thee, wherever I abide;
The first my thought, the other my desire,
These present-absent with swift motion slide.   4
For when these quicker elements are gone
In tender embassy of love to thee,
My life, being made of four, with two alone
Sinks down to death, oppressed with melancholy;   8
Until life's composition be recured
By those swift messengers returned from thee,
Who even but now come back again, assured
Of thy fair health, recounting it to me.   12
    This told, I joy; but then no longer glad,
    I send them back again and straight grow sad.

1 *two* i.e. elements; *slight* insubstantial   4 *present-absent* now here, now
there   7 *life* living body   8 *melancholy* (induced by an excess of particular
elements or 'humors,' in this case earth and water)   9 *composition* proper
balance; *recured* restored   10 *messengers* i.e. fire and air

46

Mine eye and heart are at a mortal war
How to divide the conquest of thy sight;
Mine eye my heart thy picture's sight would bar,
4 My heart mine eye the freedom of that right.
My heart doth plead that thou in him dost lie,
A closet never pierced with crystal eyes;
But the defendant doth that plea deny
8 And says in him thy fair appearance lies.
To 'cide this title is impanellèd
A quest of thoughts, all tenants to the heart,
And by their verdict is determinèd
12 The clear eye's moiety and the dear heart's part:
    As thus: mine eye's due is thy outward part,
    And my heart's right thy inward love of heart.

2 *conquest . . . sight* i.e. spoils, consisting of the sight of you 3 *bar* deny
4 *freedom* free exercise 9 *'cide* decide 10 *quest* jury; *tenants to* i.e. from
the holdings of 12 *moiety* share

47

Betwixt mine eye and heart a league is took,
And each doth good turns now unto the other:
When that mine eye is famished for a look,
Or heart in love with sighs himself doth smother,   4
With my love's picture then my eye doth feast
And to the painted banquet bids my heart;
Another time mine eye is my heart's guest
And in his thoughts of love doth share a part.   8
So, either by thy picture or my love,
Thyself away are present still with me;
For thou not farther than my thoughts canst move,
And I am still with them, and they with thee;   12
    Or, if they sleep, thy picture in my sight
    Awakes my heart to heart's and eye's delight.

1 *a league is took* an agreement is reached   6 *painted banquet* i.e. visual feast   12 *still* always

48

How careful was I, when I took my way,
Each trifle under truest bars to thrust,
That to my use it might unusèd stay
4   From hands of falsehood, in sure wards of trust!
But thou, to whom my jewels trifles are,
Most worthy comfort, now my greatest grief,
Thou best of dearest, and mine only care,
8   Art left the prey of every vulgar thief.
Thee have I not locked up in any chest,
Save where thou art not, though I feel thou art,
Within the gentle closure of my breast,
12   From whence at pleasure thou mayst come and part;
    And even thence thou wilt be stol'n, I fear,
    For truth proves thievish for a prize so dear.

1 *took my way* set out on my journey   4 *hands of falsehood* thieves   5 *to* in comparison with; *jewels* prized material possessions   7 *only care* only thing valued   8 *vulgar* common   11 *closure* enclosure   14 *truth* i.e. truth (honesty) itself

49

Against that time, if ever that time come,
When I shall see thee frown on my defects,
Whenas thy love hath cast his utmost sum,
Called to that audit by advised respects;   4
Against that time when thou shalt strangely pass
And scarcely greet me with that sun, thine eye,
When love, converted from the thing it was,
Shall reasons find of settled gravity: 8
Against that time do I ensconce me here
Within the knowledge of mine own desert,
And this my hand against myself uprear
To guard the lawful reasons on thy part.   12
    To leave poor me thou hast the strength of laws,
    Since why to love I can allege no cause.

---

1 *Against* in provision for   3 *Whenas* when; *cast . . . sum* made its final reckoning   4 *advised respects* considered reasons   5 *strangely* like a stranger   8 *of settled gravity* for continued coldness (?), of sufficient weight (?)   9 *ensconce* fortify   11–12 *this . . . part* i.e. swear, to my own disadvantage, that your actions are lawful   14 *cause* i.e. lawful obligation

50

How heavy do I journey on the way
When what I seek (my weary travel's end)
Doth teach that ease and that repose to say,
4   'Thus far the miles are measured from thy friend.'
The beast that bears me, tired with my woe,
Plods dully on, to bear that weight in me,
As if by some instinct the wretch did know
8   His rider loved not speed, being made from thee.
The bloody spur cannot provoke him on
That sometimes anger thrusts into his hide,
Which heavily he answers with a groan,
12   More sharp to me than spurring to his side;
    For that same groan doth put this in my mind:
    My grief lies onward and my joy behind.

1 *heavy* sadly   2–3 *When . . . say* i.e. when the longed-for journey's end will bring, along with its ease and repose, the reminder that   12 *sharp* painful

51

Thus can my love excuse the slow offense
Of my dull bearer when from thee I speed:
From where thou art why should I haste me thence?
Till I return, of posting is no need.   4
O, what excuse will my poor beast then find
When swift extremity can seem but slow?
Then should I spur, though mounted on the wind,
In wingèd speed no motion shall I know.   8
Then can no horse with my desire keep pace;
Therefore desire, of perfect'st love being made,
Shall weigh no dull flesh in his fiery race;
But love, for love, thus shall excuse my jade: 12
    Since from thee going he went wilful slow,
    Towards thee I'll run and give him leave to go.

---

1 *slow offense* tardiness   4 *posting* riding in haste   6 *swift extremity* extreme swiftness   8 *know* recognize   11 *weigh* consider (?), bear (?) (emendation of 'naigh' in Q)   12 *for love* for love's sake (?)   14 *go* walk

52

So am I as the rich whose blessèd key
Can bring him to his sweet up-lockèd treasure,
The which he will not ev'ry hour survey,
4   For blunting the fine point of seldom pleasure.
Therefore are feasts so solemn and so rare,
Since, seldom coming, in the long year set,
Like stones of worth they thinly placèd are,
8   Or captain jewels in the carcanet.
So is the time that keeps you as my chest,
Or as the wardrobe which the robe doth hide,
To make some special instant special blest
12   By new unfolding his imprisoned pride.
    Blessèd are you, whose worthiness gives scope,
    Being had, to triumph, being lacked, to hope.

4 *For* for fear of; *seldom pleasure* pleasure seldom enjoyed   8 *captain* chief;
carcanet jewelled collar 9 *as* like 12 *his* its

53

What is your substance, whereof are you made,
That millions of strange shadows on you tend?
Since every one hath, every one, one shade,
And you, but one, can every shadow lend.   4
Describe Adonis, and the counterfeit
Is poorly imitated after you.
On Helen's cheek all art of beauty set,
And you in Grecian tires are painted new.   8
Speak of the spring and foison of the year:
The one doth shadow of your beauty show,
The other as your bounty doth appear,
And you in every blessèd shape we know.   12
    In all external grace you have some part,
     But you like none, none you, for constant heart.

2 *strange shadows* foreign shades (Venus, Adonis, etc.); *tend* attend **4** *And . . . lend* i.e. each *shadow* can reflect but one of your excellences (with *you* the object of *lend*) **5** *counterfeit* picture **8** *tires* attire **9** *foison* harvest

54

O, how much more doth beauty beauteous seem
By that sweet ornament which truth doth give:
The rose looks fair, but fairer we it deem
For that sweet odor which doth in it live.
The canker blooms have full as deep a dye
As the perfumèd tincture of the roses,
Hang on such thorns, and play as wantonly
When summer's breath their maskèd buds discloses;
But, for their virtue only is their show,
They live unwooed and unrespected fade,
Die to themselves. Sweet roses do not so:
Of their sweet deaths are sweetest odors made.
    And so of you, beauteous and lovely youth,
    When that shall vade, my verse distills your truth.

2 *By* by means of   5 *canker blooms* dog-roses   6 *tincture* color   7 *wantonly* sportively   8 *maskèd* hidden   9 *for* since   14 *vade* depart; *distills your truth* i.e. preserves your essence as a distillation

55

Not marble nor the gilded monuments
Of princes shall outlive this pow'rful rime,
But you shall shine more bright in these contents
Than unswept stone, besmeared with sluttish time.   4
When wasteful war shall statues overturn,
And broils root out the work of masonry,
Nor Mars his sword nor war's quick fire shall burn
The living record of your memory.   8
'Gainst death and all oblivious enmity
Shall you pace forth; your praise shall still find room
Even in the eyes of all posterity
That wear this world out to the ending doom.   12
    So, till the judgment that yourself arise,
    You live in this, and dwell in lovers' eyes.

2 *rime* poem 3 *these contents* what is here contained 4 *Than* than in; *stone* memorial tablet; *sluttish* untidy 6 *broils* battles 7 *Nor* neither; *Mars his sword* i.e. the sword of Mars shall destroy 9 *all oblivious enmity* i.e. oblivion the enemy of all 12 *That wear* who last 13 *judgment that* judgment day when

56

Sweet love, renew thy force; be it not said
Thy edge should blunter be than appetite,
Which but to-day by feeding is allayed,
4   To-morrow sharp'ned in his former might.
So, love, be thou: although to-day thou fill
Thy hungry eyes even till they wink with fulness,
To-morrow see again, and do not kill
8   The spirit of love with a perpetual dulness.
Let this sad int'rim like the ocean be
Which parts the shore where two contracted new
Come daily to the banks, that, when they see
12   Return of love, more blest may be the view;
    Or call it winter, which, being full of care,
    Makes summer's welcome thrice more wished, more rare.

1 *love* spirit of love 2 *appetite* lust 4 *sharp'ned in* sharpened to **6** *wink* shut 9 *sad int'rim* lamentable interval 10 *parts the shore* divides the shores; *contracted new* newly betrothed 12 *love* the loved one

57

Being your slave, what should I do but tend
Upon the hours and times of your desire?
I have no precious time at all to spend,
Nor services to do till you require.   4
Nor dare I chide the world-without-end hour
Whilst I, my sovereign, watch the clock for you,
Nor think the bitterness of absence sour
When you have bid your servant once adieu.   8
Nor dare I question with my jealious thought
Where you may be, or your affairs suppose,
But, like a sad slave, stay and think of nought
Save where you are how happy you make those.   12
    So true a fool is love that in your will,
    Though you do anything, he thinks no ill.

---

5 *world-without-end* tedious, everlasting   9 *question* dispute; *jealious* jealous   10 *suppose* speculate about   11 *sad* sober

58

That god forbid that made me first your slave
I should in thought control your times of pleasure,
Or at your hand th' account of hours to crave,
4 Being your vassal bound to stay your leisure.
O, let me suffer, being at your beck,
Th' imprisoned absence of your liberty;
And patience, tame to sufferance, bide each check
8 Without accusing you of injury.
Be where you list; your charter is so strong
That you yourself may privilege your time
To what you will; to you it doth belong
12 Yourself to pardon of self-doing crime.
  I am to wait, though waiting so be hell,
  Not blame your pleasure, be it ill or well.

3 *th' account of* an accounting for; *to crave* should crave 4 *stay* await **6** *Th' . . . liberty* i.e. the imprisonment that your freedom-to-be-absent brings 7 *tame to sufferance* trained to accept suffering; *bide each check* put up with each rebuke 9 *list* wish; *charter* privilege 10 *privilege* dispose of, assign 12 *self-doing* done by yourself

59

If there be nothing new, but that which is
Hath been before, how are our brains beguiled,
Which, laboring for invention, bear amiss
The second burden of a former child!   4
O that record could with a backward look,
Even of five hundred courses of the sun,
Show me your image in some antique book,
Since mind at first in character was done: 8
That I might see what the old world could say
To this composèd wonder of your frame;
Whether we are mended, or whe'r better they,
Or whether revolution be the same.   12
    O, sure I am the wits of former days
    To subjects worse have given admiring praise.

1 *that* everything   3 *invention* novelty   3–4 *bear . . . of* i.e. merely mis-carry   5 *record* memory   6 *courses . . . sun* years   8 *Since . . . done* since thought was first expressed in writing   10 *composèd wonder* wonderful composition   11 *mended* improved; *whe'r* whether   12 *revolution . . . same* one cycle repeats another

60

Like as the waves make towards the pebbled shore,
So do our minutes hasten to their end;
Each changing place with that which goes before,
In sequent toil all forwards do contend
Nativity, once in the main of light,
Crawls to maturity, wherewith being crowned,
Crooked eclipses 'gainst his glory fight,
And Time that gave doth now his gift confound.
Time doth transfix the flourish set on youth
And delves the parallels in beauty's brow,
Feeds on the rarities of nature's truth,
And nothing stands but for his scythe to mow:
    And yet to times in hope my verse shall stand,
    Praising thy worth, despite his cruel hand

4 *sequent* successive; *contend* struggle   5 *Nativity* the new-born; *the . . . light* orbit   7 *Crooked* adverse, malignant   8 *confound* destroy   10 *delves the parallels* digs the lines   13 *times in hope* hoped-for times; *stand* endure

61

Is it thy will thy image should keep open
My heavy eyelids to the weary night?
Dost thou desire my slumbers should be broken
While shadows like to thee do mock my sight?   4
Is it thy spirit that thou send'st from thee
So far from home into my deeds to pry,
To find out shames and idle hours in me,
The scope and tenure of thy jealousy?   8
O no, thy love, though much, is not so great;
It is my love that keeps mine eye awake,
Mine own true love that doth my rest defeat
To play the watchman ever for thy sake.   12
    For thee watch I whilst thou dost wake elsewhere,
    From me far off, with others all too near.

7 *shames* faults   8 *scope and tenure* aim and purport   11 *defeat* destroy

62

Sin of self-love possesseth all mine eye
And all my soul and all my every part;
And for this sin there is no remedy,
4   It is so grounded inward in my heart.
Methinks no face so gracious is as mine,
No shape so true, no truth of such account,
And for myself mine own worth do define
8   As I all other in all worths surmount.
But when my glass shows me myself indeed,
Beated and chopped with tanned antiquity,
Mine own self-love quite contrary I read;
12   Self so self-loving were iniquity:
      'Tis thee (myself) that for myself I praise,
      Painting my age with beauty of thy days.

5 *gracious* pleasing   8 *As* as if; *other* others   10 *chopped* seamed; *tanned antiquity* i.e. leathery old age   11 *contrary* in a different way   13 *'Tis . . . praise* i.e. I am praising you whom I identify with myself

63

Against my love shall be as I am now,
With Time's injurious hand crushed and o'erworn;
When hours have drained his blood and filled his brow
With lines and wrinkles, when his youthful morn   4
Hath travelled on to age's steepy night,
And all those beauties whereof now he's king
Are vanishing, or vanished out of sight,
Stealing away the treasure of his spring –   8
For such a time do I now fortify
Against confounding age's cruel knife,
That he shall never cut from memory
My sweet love's beauty, though my lover's life.   12
    His beauty shall in these black lines be seen,
    And they shall live, and he in them still green.

1 *Against* in expectation of the time when   5 *steepy* deep, precipitous   9 *fortify* build defenses   10 *confounding* destroying   12 *though* i.e. though he cuts

64

When I have seen by Time's fell hand defaced
The rich proud cost of outworn buried age,
When sometime lofty towers I see down-rased
4   And brass eternal slave to mortal rage;
When I have seen the hungry ocean gain
Advantage on the kingdom of the shore,
And the firm soil win of the wat'ry main,
8   Increasing store with loss and loss with store;
When I have seen such interchange of state,
Or state itself confounded to decay,
Ruin hath taught me thus to ruminate,
12   That Time will come and take my love away.
     This thought is as a death, which cannot choose
     But weep to have that which it fears to lose.

2 *cost* outlay   3 *sometime* formerly   4 *brass eternal* everlasting brass;
mortal rage ravages of mortality   6 *Advantage* inroads   8 *Increasing . . .*
store i.e. one gaining by the other's loss, one losing by the other's gain   10
confounded reduced   14 *to have* for having

65

Since brass, nor stone, nor earth, nor boundless sea,
But sad mortality o'ersways their power,
How with this rage shall beauty hold a plea,
Whose action is no stronger than a flower?   4
O, how shall summer's honey breath hold out
Against the wrackful siege of batt'ring days,
When rocks impregnable are not so stout,
Nor gates of steel so strong but Time decays?   8
O fearful meditation: where, alack,
Shall Time's best jewel from Time's chest lie hid?
Or what strong hand can hold his swift foot back,
Or who his spoil of beauty can forbid?   12
 O, none, unless this miracle have might,
 That in black ink my love may still shine bright.

---

1 *Since* since there is neither 3 *rage* destructive power; *hold* maintain
4 *action* case 6 *wrackful* wrecking 10 *from Time's chest* i.e. from being
coffered up by Time 12 *spoil* spoliation

66

Tired with all these, for restful death I cry:
As, to behold desert a beggar born,
And needy nothing trimmed in jollity,
4 And purest faith unhappily forsworn,
And gilded honor shamefully misplaced,
And maiden virtue rudely strumpeted,
And right perfection wrongfully disgraced,
8 And strength by limping sway disablèd,
And art made tongue-tied by authority,
And folly (doctor-like) controlling skill,
And simple truth miscalled simplicity,
12 And captive good attending captain ill.
   Tired with all these, from these would I be gone,
   Save that, to die, I leave my love alone.

2 *As* such as, for instance   3 *needy . . . jollity* i.e. the lack-all nobody festively attired   4 *unhappily forsworn* evilly betrayed   7 *disgraced* banished from favor   8 *by . . . disablèd* i.e. weakened by incompetent leadership   9 *art . . . authority* (possibly an allusion to state censorship of literature)   10 *doctor-like* i.e. owlishly   11 *simplicity* stupidity

67

Ah, wherefore with infection should he live
And with his presence grace impiety,
That sin by him advantage should achieve
And lace itself with his society?   4
Why should false painting imitate his cheek
And steal dead seeing of his living hue?
Why should poor beauty indirectly seek
Roses of shadow, since his rose is true?   8
Why should he live, now Nature bankrout is,
Beggared of blood to blush through lively veins,
For she hath no exchequer now but his,
And, proud of many, lives upon his gains?   12
    O, him she stores, to show what wealth she had
    In days long since, before these last so bad.

1 *wherefore* why; *infection* corruption   3 *advantage* profit   4 *lace* i.e.
ornament   6 *dead seeing* the lifeless appearance   7 *poor* inferior; *indirectly*
by imitation   8 *Roses of shadow* i.e. pictured roses   9 *bankrout* bankrupt
10 *Beggared . . . veins* i.e. lacking the blood to blush naturally instead of by
the use of cosmetics   11 *exchequer* i.e. treasury of natural beauty   12
proud falsely proud (?)   13 *stores* preserves

68

Thus is his cheek the map of days outworn
When beauty lived and died as flowers do now,
Before these bastard signs of fair were born
4   Or durst inhabit on a living brow;
Before the golden tresses of the dead,
The right of sepulchers, were shorn away
To live a second life on second head,
8   Ere beauty's dead fleece made another gay:
In him those holy antique hours are seen,
Without all ornament, itself and true,
Making no summer of another's green,
12   Robbing no old to dress his beauty new;
    And him as for a map doth Nature store,
    To show false Art what beauty was of yore.

1 *map* representation; *outworn* outlived   3 *bastard signs* i.e. cosmetics; *fair* beauty   4 *inhabit* dwell   6 *The right of* belonging properly to   9 *antique hours* ancient times   13 *as . . . map* i.e. as if for a guide; *store* preserve

69

Those parts of thee that the world's eye doth view
Want nothing that the thought of hearts can mend;
All tongues, the voice of souls, give thee that due,
Utt'ring bare truth, even so as foes commend.   4
Thy outward thus with outward praise is crowned,
But those same tongues that give thee so thine own
In other accents do this praise confound
By seeing farther than the eye hath shown.   8
They look into the beauty of thy mind,
And that in guess they measure by thy deeds;
Then, churls, their thoughts, although their eyes were kind,
To thy fair flower add the rank smell of weeds: 12
    But why thy odor matcheth not thy show,
    The soil is this, that thou dost common grow.

1 *parts* outward parts   4 *as foes commend* i.e. forced to the admission
6 *thine own* what is due you   7 *confound* destroy   10 *in guess* at a guess
13 *odor matcheth not* (cf. Sonnet 54)   14 *soil* (1) ground, (2) soilure; *common* (1) uncultivated, like weeds, (2) overfamiliar

70

That thou art blamed shall not be thy defect,
For slander's mark was ever yet the fair;
The ornament of beauty is suspect,
4   A crow that flies in heaven's sweetest air.
So thou be good, slander doth but approve
Thy worth the greater, being wooed of time;
For canker vice the sweetest buds doth love,
8   And thou present'st a pure unstainèd prime.
Thou hast passed by the ambush of young days,
Either not assailed, or victor being charged;
Yet this thy praise cannot be so thy praise
12   To tie up envy, evermore enlarged:
    If some suspect of ill masked not thy show,
    Then thou alone kingdoms of hearts shouldst owe.

1 *defect* fault   3 *ornament* (like a 'beauty mark'); *suspect* suspicion   5 *approve* prove   6 *wooed of time* solicited to evil by the times (?)   7 *canker* destructive worm   9 *ambush* i.e. dangerous lure, trap   10 *charged* assailed   12 *tie up envy* i.e. silence malice   13 *If . . . show* i.e. if some suspicion did not obscure your fine appearance   14 *owe* own

71

No longer mourn for me when I am dead
Than you shall hear the surly sullen bell
Give warning to the world that I am fled
From this vile world, with vilest worms to dwell.   4
Nay, if you read this line, remember not
The hand that writ it, for I love you so
That I in your sweet thoughts would be forgot
If thinking on me then should make you woe.   8
O, if, I say, you look upon this verse
When I, perhaps, compounded am with clay,
Do not so much as my poor name rehearse,
But let your love even with my life decay,   12
    Lest the wise world should look into your moan
    And mock you with me after I am gone.

8 *make you woe* make woe for you   10 *compounded* blended   13 *wise* i.e.
disdainful of foolish sentiment   14 *with* because of

72

O, lest the world should task you to recite
What merit lived in me that you should love
After my death, dear love, forget me quite,
4 For you in me can nothing worthy prove;
Unless you would devise some virtuous lie,
To do more for me than mine own desert
And hang more praise upon deceasèd I
8 Than niggard truth would willingly impart.
O, lest your true love may seem false in this,
That you for love speak well of me untrue,
My name be buried where my body is,
12 And live no more to shame nor me nor you;
    For I am shamed by that which I bring forth,
    And so should you, to love things nothing worth.

1 *task . . . recite* put you to the task of telling   5 *virtuous lie* noble lie (?), false attribution of virtue (?)   8 *niggard* miserly   10 *untrue* untruly   12 *nor . . . nor* either . . . or   13 *which . . . forth* (probably a deprecatory allusion to the sonnets)

73

That time of year thou mayst in me behold
When yellow leaves, or none, or few, do hang
Upon those boughs which shake against the cold,
Bare ruined choirs where late the sweet birds sang   4
In me thou seest the twilight of such day
As after sunset fadeth in the west,
Which by and by black night doth take away,
Death's second self that seals up all in rest.   8
In me thou seest the glowing of such fire
That on the ashes of his youth doth lie,
As the deathbed whereon it must expire,
Consumed with that which it was nourished by.   12
   This thou perceiv'st, which makes thy love more strong,
   To love that well which thou must leave ere long.

4 *choirs* i.e. the part of a church or monastery where services were sung
7 *by and by* shortly   8 *seals up* encloses   10 *That* as   12 *with . . . by* i.e. by life

74

But be contented: when that fell arrest
Without all bail shall carry me away,
My life hath in this line some interest
4   Which for memorial still with thee shall stay.
When thou reviewest this, thou dost review
The very part was consecrate to thee:
The earth can have but earth, which is his due;
8   My spirit is thine, the better part of me.
So then thou hast but lost the dregs of life,
The prey of worms, my body being dead,
The coward conquest of a wretch's knife,
12   Too base of thee to be rememberèd.
    The worth of that is that which it contains,
    And that is this, and this with thee remains.

1 *fell* fatal   2 *Without all bail* i.e. irreprievably   3 *line* poem; *interest* share   4 *still* always   7 *his due* its due (i.e. 'dust to dust')   11 *The . . . knife* i.e. easily cut down by the bravo Death (?)   13–14 *The worth . . . is this* i.e. the only value of the body is as a container of the soul, and the soul is in this poem

75

So are you to my thoughts as food to life,
Or as sweet-seasoned showers are to the ground;
And for the peace of you I hold such strife
As 'twixt a miser and his wealth is found: 4
Now proud as an enjoyer, and anon
Doubting the filching age will steal his treasure;
Now counting best to be with you alone,
Then bettered that the world may see my pleasure; 8
Sometime all full with feasting on your sight,
And by and by clean starvèd for a look,
Possessing or pursuing no delight
Save what is had or must from you be took. 12
    Thus do I pine and surfeit day by day,
    Or gluttoning on all, or all away.

2 *sweet-seasoned* of the sweet season, spring 3 *peace of you* i.e. peace you
bring me; *hold such strife* i.e. exist on such uneasy terms 5 *anon* soon
6 *Doubting* fearing 8 *bettered* better pleased 14 *Or . . . away* i.e. either
feeding on the full feast of your presence or having nothing in your absence

76

Why is my verse so barren of new pride?
So far from variation or quick change?
Why, with the time, do I not glance aside
4   To new-found methods and to compounds strange?
Why write I still all one, ever the same,
And keep invention in a noted weed,
That every word doth almost tell my name,
8   Showing their birth, and where they did proceed?
O, know, sweet love, I always write of you,
And you and love are still my argument;
So all my best is dressing old words new,
12   Spending again what is already spent:
     For as the sun is daily new and old,
     So is my love still telling what is told.

---

1 *pride* adornment   2 *quick change* modishness   3 *the time* the times, i.e. the current styles   4 *compounds strange* i.e. literary concoctions (?), neologisms, like those being introduced by Marston (?)   5 *one* one way   6 *invention* poetic creation; *noted weed* familar garb   10 *argument* theme   11 *So...best* i.e. so that the best I am capable of

77

Thy glass will show thee how thy beauties wear,
Thy dial how thy precious minutes waste;
The vacant leaves thy mind's imprint will bear,
And of this book this learning mayst thou taste.   4
The wrinkles which thy glass will truly show,
Of mouthèd graves will give thee memory.
Thou by thy dial's shady stealth mayst know
Time's thievish progress to eternity.   8
Look what thy memory cannot contain,
Commit to these waste blanks, and thou shalt find
Those children nursed, delivered from thy brain,
To take a new acquaintance of thy mind.   12
　　These offices, so oft as thou wilt look,
　　Shall profit thee and much enrich thy book.

1 *glass* mirror; *wear* wear out   2 *dial* sun-dial   3 *vacant leaves* i.e. the blank leaves of a tablet (?) (cf. Sonnet 122); *mind's imprint* i.e. the reflections to be written in the tablet   4 *this learning* i.e. the wisdom brought by his own reflections   6 *mouthèd* devouring; *memory* reminder   8 *thievish* stealthy   9 *Look what* whatever   10 *waste blanks* blank pages   11 *nursed* preserved   13 *offices* regular duties; *look* i.e. at the glass, the dial, and what has been previously written in the book

78

So oft have I invoked thee for my Muse
And found such fair assistance in my verse
As every alien pen hath got my use
4   And under thee their poesy disperse.
Thine eyes, that taught the dumb on high to sing
And heavy ignorance aloft to fly,
Have added feathers to the learnèd's wing
8   And given grace a double majesty.
Yet be most proud of that which I compile,
Whose influence is thine and born of thee.
In others' works thou dost but mend the style,
12   And arts with thy sweet graces gracèd be;
But thou art all my art and dost advance
As high as learning my rude ignorance.

3 *As* that; *alien* i.e. belonging to outsiders; *got my use* followed my practise
4 *under thee* i.e. with you as their Muse   5 *on high* in exultation (like the
lark)   7 *added feathers* i.e. imped their wings for still higher flights   8 *grace*
(an attribute of majesty)   10 *Whose . . . thine* i.e. wholly inspired by you
11 *mend* i.e. merely improve

79

Whilst I alone did call upon thy aid,
My verse alone had all thy gentle grace;
But now my gracious numbers are decayed,
And my sick Muse doth give another place.　　4
I grant, sweet love, thy lovely argument
Deserves the travail of a worthier pen;
Yet what of thee thy poet doth invent
He robs thee of, and pays it thee again.　　8
He lends thee virtue, and he stole that word
From thy behavior; beauty doth he give,
And found it in thy cheek: he can afford
No praise to thee but what in thee doth live.　　12
　　Then thank him not for that which he doth say,
　　Since what he owes thee thou thyself dost pay.

4 *give another place* yield place to another　5 *thy lovely argument* the theme of your loveliness　11 *afford* offer　14 *owes* is obliged to give

80

O, how I faint when I of you do write,
Knowing a better spirit doth use your name
And in the praise thereof spends all his might
4   To make me tongue-tied, speaking of your fame.
But since your worth (wide as the ocean is)
The humble as the proudest sail doth bear,
My saucy bark, inferior far to his,
8   On your broad main doth wilfully appear.
Your shallowest help will hold me up afloat
Whilst he upon your soundless deep doth ride;
Or, being wracked, I am a worthless boat,
12   He of tall building and of goodly pride.
   Then if he thrive, and I be cast away,
   The worst was this: my love was my decay.

1 *faint* falter   2 *better spirit* i.e. more richly gifted poet   4 *tongue-tied* i.e. in comparison with the other   6 *as* as well as   8 *wilfully* i.e. boldly, in spite of all   10 *soundless* unfathomable   11 *wracked* wrecked; *boat* (any vessel less considerable than a ship)   12 *tall* sturdy; *pride* splendor   14 *decay* destruction

81

Or I shall live your epitaph to make,
Or you survive when I in earth am rotten.
From hence your memory death cannot take,
Although in me each part will be forgotten.   4
Your name from hence immortal life shall have,
Though I, once gone, to all the world must die.
The earth can yield me but a common grave
When you entombèd in men's eyes shall lie.   8
Your monument shall be my gentle verse,
Which eyes not yet created shall o'erread;
And tongues to be your being shall rehearse
When all the breathers of this world are dead.   12
    You still shall live (such virtue hath my pen)
    Where breath most breathes, even in the mouths of men.

1 *Or* either   3, 5 *hence* the present poems   4 *in . . . part* every part of me
8 *entombèd . . . lie* i.e kept always before their eyes   11 *rehearse* recite   13
virtue power   14 *breath* speech (?), soul (?)

82

I grant thou wert not married to my Muse
And therefore mayst without attaint o'erlook
The dedicated words which writers use
4 Of their fair subject, blessing every book.
Thou art as fair in knowledge as in hue,
Finding thy worth a limit past my praise;
And therefore art enforced to seek anew
8 Some fresher stamp of the time-bettering days.
And do so, love; yet when they have devised
What strainèd touches rhetoric can lend,
Thou, truly fair, wert truly sympathized
12 In true plain words by thy true-telling friend:
    And their gross painting might be better used
    Where cheeks need blood; in thee it is abused.

2 *attaint* dishonor; *o'erlook* peruse   3 *dedicated* devoted; *writers* i.e. other writers   5 *hue* complexion   6 *Finding . . . past* i.e. knowing your worth to extend beyond   8 *stamp* imprint; *time-bettering* improving, progressing with the times   10 *strainèd* excessive   11 *sympathized* represented   14 *abused* i.e. an abuse

83

I never saw that you did painting need,
And therefore to your fair no painting set;
I found, or thought I found, you did exceed
The barren tender of a poet's debt: 4
And therefore have I slept in your report,
That you yourself, being extant, well might show
How far a modern quill doth come too short,
Speaking of worth, what worth in you doth grow.   8
This silence for my sin you did impute,
Which shall be most my glory, being dumb,
For I impair not beauty, being mute,
When others would give life and bring a tomb.   12
    There lives more life in one of your fair eyes
    Than both your poets can in praise devise.

2 *fair* beauty; *set* applied   4 *barren tender* worthless offering; *debt* payment
5 *slept . . . report* been inactive in writing of you   7 *modern* trite   8 *Speaking*
in speaking; *what worth* i.e. to speak of such worth as   12 *bring a tomb*
bring death (i.e. by reducing your living features to a dead image)

84

Who is it that says most, which can say more
Than this rich praise, that you alône are you,
In whose confine immurèd is the store
4   Which should example where your equal grew?
Lean penury within that pen doth dwell
That to his subject lends not some small glory,
But he that writes of you, if he can tell
8   That you are you, so dignifies his story.
Let him but copy what in you is writ,
Not making worse what nature made so clear,
And such a counterpart shall fame his wit,
12   Making his style admirèd everywhere.
       You to your beauteous blessings add a curse,
       Being fond on praise, which makes your praises worse.

---

1 *Who . . . more* i.e. who that says the utmost can say more   3–4 *In . . . grew*
in whom are locked up all the qualities needed to provide an equal example
6 *his* its   8 *so* i.e. sufficiently   11 *counterpart* copy; *fame* bring fame to
14 *fond on* (probably a corruption: the *curse* would appear to be on poets,
who fail because he is beyond their praise)

85

My tongue-tied Muse in manners holds her still
While comments of your praise, richly compiled,
Reserve their character with golden quill
And precious phrase by all the Muses filed.   4
I think good thoughts whilst other write good words,
And, like unlettered clerk, still cry 'Amen'
To every hymn that able spirit affords
In polished form of well-refinèd pen.   8
Hearing you praised, I say, ''Tis so, 'tis true,'
And to the most of praise add something more;
But that is in my thought, whose love to you,
Though words come hindmost, holds his rank before.   12
    Then others for the breath of words respect;
    Me for my dumb thoughts, speaking in effect.

1 *in . . . still* i.e. politely remains silent   2–3 *While . . . character* (an obscure passage, possibly corrupt)   2 *comments* expositions (?); *compiled* composed (?)   3 *Reserve* preserve (?); *character* writing (?)   4 *filed* polished   5 *other* others   6 *unlettered clerk* illiterate parish clerk; *still* always   6–7 *cry . . . affords* i.e. give approval to every poem offered by an able poet   10 *most* utmost   13 *the . . . words* i.e. actual speech   14 *speaking in effect* i.e. virtually speaking

86

Was it the proud full sail of his great verse,
Bound for the prize of all-too-precious you,
That did my ripe thoughts in my brain inhearse,
4   Making their tomb the womb wherein they grew?
Was it his spirit, by spirits taught to write
Above a mortal pitch, that struck me dead?
No, neither he, nor his compeers by night
8   Giving him aid, my verse astonishèd.
He, nor that affable familiar ghost
Which nightly gulls him with intelligence,
As victors, of my silence cannot boast;
12   I was not sick of any fear from thence:
      But when your countenance filled up his line,
      Then lacked I matter; that enfeebled mine.

1 *his* i.e. an unidentified rival poet's   2 *Bound . . . of* i.e. designed to capture
3 *inhearse* coffin up   5 *spirits* divine inspirers   6 *dead* dead silent   7
compeers by night collaborators, spirit aids   8 *astonishèd* dumbfounded
10 *gulls . . . intelligence* tricks him with spying reports (allusion obscure)
13 *countenance filled up* approval repaired any defect in

87

Farewell: thou art too dear for my possessing,
And like enough thou know'st thy estimate.
The charter of thy worth gives thee releasing;
My bonds in thee are all determinate.   4
For how do I hold thee but by thy granting,
And for that riches where is my deserving?
The cause of this fair gift in me is wanting,
And so my patent back again is swerving.   8
Thyself thou gav'st, thy own worth then not knowing,
Or me, to whom thou gav'st it, else mistaking;
So thy great gift, upon misprision growing,
Comes home again, on better judgment making.   12
    Thus have I had thee as a dream doth flatter,
    In sleep a king, but waking no such matter.

1 *dear* precious, costly 2 *estimate* value 3 *charter* privilege; *releasing*
i.e. release from obligation 4 *bonds* claims; *determinate* ended 7 *cause*
justification; *wanting* lacking 8 *patent* right; *swerving* turning away 10
mistaking i.e. overestimating 11 *upon misprision growing* based on error
12 *on . . . making* on your coming to a better judgment 13 *as . . . flatter*
as in a flattering dream

88

When thou shalt be disposed to set me light
And place my merit in the eye of scorn,
Upon thy side against myself I'll fight
4   And prove thee virtuous, though thou art forsworn.
With mine own weakness being best acquainted,
Upon thy part I can set down a story
Of faults concealed wherein I am attainted,
8   That thou, in losing me, shall win much glory:
And by this will be a gainer too;
For, bending all my loving thoughts on thee,
The injuries that to myself I do,
12   Doing thee vantage, double-vantage me.
       Such is my love, to thee I so belong,
       That for thy right myself will bear all wrong.

1 *set me light* make light of me   7 *attainted* dishonored   8 *losing* getting rid of   10 *bending* turning   12 *vantage* advantage

89

Say that thou didst forsake me for some fault,
And I will comment upon that offense;
Speak of my lameness, and I straight will halt,
Against thy reasons making no defense.   4
Thou canst not, love, disgrace me half so ill,
To set a form upon desirèd change,
As I'll myself disgrace; knowing thy will,
I will acquaintance strangle and look strange,   8
Be absent from thy walks, and in my tongue
Thy sweet belovèd name no more shall dwell,
Lest I, too much profane, should do it wrong
And haply of our old acquaintance tell.   12
    For thee, against myself I'll vow debate,
    For I must ne'er love him whom thou dost hate.

2 *comment* expatiate 3 *lameness* i.e. defect (metaphorical); *halt* limp
4 *reasons* charges 6 *To . . . change* i.e. to seem to justify the change you
wish to make in our relationship 7 *disgrace* depreciate 8 *acquaintance*
i.e. the fact of my being acquainted with you; *strange* as a stranger 12
haply accidentally 13 *vow debate* declare war

90

Then hate me when thou wilt; if ever, now;
Now, while the world is bent my deeds to cross,
Join with the spite of fortune, make me bow,
4 And do not drop in for an after-loss.
Ah, do not, when my heart hath scaped this sorrow,
Come in the rearward of a conquered woe;
Give not a windy night a rainy morrow,
8 To linger out a purposed overthrow.
If thou wilt leave me, do not leave me last,
When other petty griefs have done their spite,
But in the onset come: so shall I taste
12 At first the very worst of fortune's might;
    And other strains of woe, which now seem woe,
    Compared with loss of thee will not seem so.

2 *bent* determined; *cross* thwart   4 *drop . . . after-loss* i.e. casually add
to my griefs later on   5 *scaped* escaped   6 *Come . . . woe* i.e. attack after I
have overcome my sorrow   8 *linger out* protract; *purposed* predestined
13 *strains* kinds

91

Some glory in their birth, some in their skill,
Some in their wealth, some in their body's force,
Some in their garments, though newfangled ill,
Some in their hawks and hounds, some in their horse;   **4**
And every humor hath his adjunct pleasure,
Wherein it finds a joy above the rest,
But these particulars are not my measure;
All these I better in one general best.   **8**
Thy love is better than high birth to me,
Richer than wealth, prouder than garments' cost,
Of more delight than hawks or horses be;
And having thee, of all men's pride I boast: **12**
    Wretched in this alone, that thou mayst take
    All this away and me most wretched make.

2 *force* strength   **3** *newfangled ill* modishly ugly   **4** *horse* horses   **5** *humor* disposition; *his* its; *adjunct* corresponding   **7** *particulars* i.e. various possessions; *measure* standard of happiness   **8** *better* improve upon   **12** *all men's pride* i.e. all the things that men take pride in

92

But do thy worst to steal thyself away,
For term of life thou art assurèd mine,
And life no longer than thy love will stay,
For it depends upon that love of thine.
Then need I not to fear the worst of wrongs
When in the least of them my life hath end;
I see a better state to me belongs
Than that which on thy humor doth depend.
Thou canst not vex me with inconstant mind,
Since that my life on thy revolt doth lie.
O, what a happy title do I find,
Happy to have thy love, happy to die!
    But what's so blessèd-fair that fears no blot?
    Thou mayst be false, and yet I know it not.

2 *term of life* my lifetime   5–6 *Then . . . end* i.e. there is no distinction in misfortunes since there is really only one – the loss of friendship, which ends life   8 *humor* whim   10 *on thy . . . lie* i.e. ends with your turning away from me   11 *happy title* title to happiness   14 *Thou . . . not* i.e. I may be denied the releasing death which certainty of your falsehood would bring

93

So shall I live, supposing thou art true,
Like a deceivèd husband; so love's face
May still seem love to me though altered new,
Thy looks with me, thy heart in other place.   4
For there can live no hatred in thine eye;
Therefore in that I cannot know thy change;
In many's looks the false heart's history
Is writ in moods and frowns and wrinkles strange: 8
But heaven in thy creation did decree
That in thy face sweet love should ever dwell;
Whate'er thy thoughts or thy heart's workings be,
Thy looks should nothing thence but sweetness tell.   12
    How like Eve's apple doth thy beauty grow
    If thy sweet virtue answer not thy show!

---

2 *face* appearance   8 *moods* looks of moodiness; *strange* unaccustomed
12 *thence* i.e. by themselves   13 *Eve's apple* i.e. fair only in appearance;
grow become

94

They that have pow'r to hurt and will do none,
That do not do the thing they most do show,
Who, moving others, are themselves as stone,
4   Unmovèd, cold, and to temptation slow;
They rightly do inherit heaven's graces
And husband nature's riches from expense;
They are the lords and owners of their faces,
8   Others but stewards of their excellence.
The summer's flow'r is to the summer sweet,
Though to itself it only live and die;
But if that flow'r with base infection meet,
12   The basest weed outbraves his dignity:
    For sweetest things turn sourest by their deeds;
    Lilies that fester smell far worse than weeds.

1 *and . . . none* i.e. without actively trying to hurt   2 *show* i.e. seem to do, or seem capable of doing   5 *rightly* as a right, veritably   6 *expense* expenditure   7 *owners . . . faces* permanent possessors of the qualities that show in them   8 *stewards* dispensers   12 *outbraves his* outglories its   14 *Lilies . . . weeds* (this line also appears in the anonymous play *Edward III*, pub. 1596, ed. 1897, II, i, 451, in one of the scenes frequently attributed to Shakespeare)

95

How sweet and lovely dost thou make the shame
Which, like a canker in the fragrant rose,
Doth spot the beauty of thy budding name!
O, in what sweets dost thou thy sins enclose!   4
That tongue that tells the story of thy days,
Making lascivious comments on thy sport,
Cannot dispraise but in a kind of praise;
Naming thy name blesses an ill report.   8
O, what a mansion have those vices got
Which for their habitation chose out thee,
Where beauty's veil doth cover every blot
And all things turns to fair that eyes can see!   12
    Take heed, dear heart, of this large privilege;
    The hardest knife ill used doth lose his edge.

2 *canker* worm   3 *name* reputation   5 *thy days* i.e. how you spend your
days   6 *sport* amours   9 *mansion* dwelling   14 *his* its

96

Some say thy fault is youth, some wantonness;
Some say thy grace is youth and gentle sport;
Both grace and faults are loved of more and less:
4   Thou mak'st faults graces that to thee resort.
As on the finger of a thronèd queen
The basest jewel will be well esteemed,
So are those errors that in thee are seen
8   To truths translated and for true things deemed.
How many lambs might the stern wolf betray
If like a lamb he could his looks translate!
How many gazers mightst thou lead away
12   If thou wouldst use the strength of all thy state!
      But do not so; I love thee in such sort
      As, thou being mine, mine is thy good report.

1 *wantonness* amorous dalliance (the *gentle sport* of l. 2)   3 *of more and less* by great and small   8 *translated* transformed   9 *stern* cruel   12 *state* power   13–14 *But . . . report* (the same couplet ends Sonnet 36)

97

How like a winter hath my absence been
From thee, the pleasure of the fleeting year!
What freezings have I felt, what dark days seen!
What old December's bareness everywhere!   4
And yet this time removed was summer's time,
The teeming autumn, big with rich increase,
Bearing the wanton burden of the prime,
Like widowed wombs after their lords' decease: 8
Yet this abundant issue seemed to me
But hope of orphans and unfathered fruit;
For summer and his pleasures wait on thee,
And, thou away, the very birds are mute;   12
   Or, if they sing, 'tis with so dull a cheer
   That leaves look pale, dreading the winter's near.

2 *pleasure* i.e. pleasant portion **5** *removed* i.e. when I was absent **6**
teeming fertile; *increase* harvest **7** *wanton burden* i.e. fruit of wantonness;
prime spring **9** *issue* progeny **10** *hope of orphans* orphaned hope **11**
his its

98

From you have I been absent in the spring,
When proud-pied April, dressed in all his trim,
Hath put a spirit of youth in everything,
4   That heavy Saturn laughed and leapt with him;
Yet nor the lays of birds, nor the sweet smell
Of different flowers in odor and in hue,
Could make me any summer's story tell,
8   Or from their proud lap pluck them where they grew:
Nor did I wonder at the lily's white,
Nor praise the deep vermilion in the rose;
They were but sweet, but figures of delight,
12   Drawn after you, you pattern of all those.
      Yet seemed it winter still, and you away,
      As with your shadow I with these did play.

2 *proud-pied* gloriously dappled; *trim* ornament 4 *heavy Saturn* (the melancholy planet) 5 *nor . . . nor* neither . . . nor; *lays* songs 6 *different flowers* flowers different 7 *summer's* summery, gay 8 *proud lap* i.e. mother earth 11 *figures* emblems 14 *shadow* portrait

99

The forward violet thus did I chide:
Sweet thief, whence didst thou steal thy sweet that smells,
If not from my love's breath? The purple pride
Which on thy soft cheek for complexion dwells   4
In my love's veins thou hast too grossly dyed.
The lily I condemnèd for thy hand;
And buds of marjoram had stol'n thy hair;
The roses fearfully on thorns did stand,   8
One blushing shame, another white despair;
A third, nor red nor white, had stol'n of both,
And to his robb'ry had annexed thy breath;
But, for his theft, in pride of all his growth   12
A vengeful canker eat him up to death.
    More flowers I noted, yet I none could see
    But sweet or color it had stol'n from thee.

---

1 *forward* early **3** *pride* splendor **5** *grossly* obviously **6** *condemnèd for*
i.e. found guilty of stealing the color of **11** *annexed* compounded the theft
of **13** *canker eat* worm ate **15** *sweet* scent

100

Where art thou, Muse, that thou forget'st so long
To speak of that which gives thee all thy might?
Spend'st thou thy fury on some worthless song,
4   Dark'ning thy pow'r to lend base subjects light?
Return, forgetful Muse, and straight redeem
In gentle numbers time so idly spent;
Sing to the ear that doth thy lays esteem
8   And gives thy pen both skill and argument.
Rise, resty Muse, my love's sweet face survey,
If Time have any wrinkle graven there;
If any, be a satire to decay
12   And make Time's spoils despisèd everywhere.
    Give my love fame faster than Time wastes life;
    So thou prevent'st his scythe and crooked knife.

3 *fury* poetic frenzy   4 *Dark'ning* diminishing   6 *gentle numbers* noble
verses   9 *resty* lazy   11 *be a satire to* satirize   14 *thou prevent'st* you thwart

IOI

O truant Muse, what shall be thy amends
For thy neglect of truth in beauty dyed?
Both truth and beauty on my love depends;
So dost thou too, and therein dignified.   4
Make answer, Muse: wilt thou not haply say,
'Truth needs no color with his color fixed,
Beauty no pencil, beauty's truth to lay;
But best is best, if never intermixed.'   8
Because he needs no praise, wilt thou be dumb?
Excuse not silence so, for't lies in thee
To make him much outlive a gilded tomb
And to be praised of ages yet to be.   12
　　　Then do thy office, Muse; I teach thee how
　　　To make him seem, long hence, as he shows now.

---

2 *dyed* stamped   **4** *thou* i.e. his Muse; *dignified* you are dignified   **5** *haply* perchance   **6** *no color* no artificial coloring; *his color fixed* its natural and permanent color   **7** *lay* lay on   **8** *intermixed* i.e. with true and false inter-mingled   **13** *do thy office* perform your function

102

My love is strength'ned, though more weak in seeming;
I love not less, though less the show appear:
That love is merchandized whose rich esteeming
4   The owner's tongue doth publish everywhere.
Our love was new, and then but in the spring,
When I was wont to greet it with my lays,
As Philomel in summer's front doth sing
8   And stops her pipe in growth of riper days;
Not that the summer is less pleasant now
Than when her mournful hymns did hush the night,
But that wild music burdens every bough,
12   And sweets grown common lose their dear delight.
     Therefore, like her, I sometime hold my tongue,
     Because I would not dull you with my song.

---

1 *seeming* outward appearance 3 *merchandized* bartered; *esteeming* valuation 7 *Philomel* the nightingale; *front* forefront, beginning 8 *riper* later, more mature 11 *But . . . music* but because a wealth of bird-song 14 *dull* cloy, surfeit

103

Alack, what poverty my Muse brings forth,
That, having such a scope to show her pride,
The argument all bare is of more worth
Than when it hath my added praise beside. 4
O, blame me not if I no more can write!
Look in your glass, and there appears a face
That overgoes my blunt invention quite,
Dulling my lines and doing me disgrace. 8
Were it not sinful then, striving to mend,
To mar the subject that before was well?
For to no other pass my verses tend
Than of your graces and your gifts to tell; 12
    And more, much more, than in my verse can sit
    Your own glass shows you when you look in it.

---

1 *poverty* inferior stuff 2 *pride* splendor 3 *argument* theme 7 *overgoes*
outdoes; *blunt invention* crude creation 8 *Dulling* i.e. by comparison
11 *pass* purpose 13 *sit* reside

104

To me, fair friend, you never can be old,
For as you were when first your eye I eyed,
Such seems your beauty still. Three winters cold
4   Have from the forests shook three summers' pride,
Three beauteous springs to yellow autumn turned
In process of the seasons have I seen,
Three April perfumes in three hot Junes burned,
8   Since first I saw you fresh, which yet are green.
Ah, yet doth beauty, like a dial hand,
Steal from his figure, and no pace perceived;
So your sweet hue, which methinks still doth stand,
12   Hath motion, and mine eye may be deceived;
    For fear of which, hear this, thou age unbred:
    Ere you were born was beauty's summer dead.

6 *process* the progress **7** *burned* (as incense) **9** *dial* watch **10** *his figure* (1) the dial's numeral, (2) the friend's form; *and . . . perceived* i.e. with invisible movement **11** *sweet hue* fair aspect; *still* (1) motionless, unchanged, (2) always; *stand* remain constant **13** *unbred* unborn **14** *summer* i.e. peak (the friend)

105

Let not my love be called idolatry,
Nor my belovèd as an idol show,
Since all alike my songs and praises be
To one, of one, still such, and ever so.   4
Kind is my love to-day, to-morrow kind,
Still constant in a wondrous excellence;
Therefore my verse, to constancy confined,
One thing expressing, leaves out difference.   8
'Fair, kind, and true' is all my argument,
'Fair, kind, and true,' varying to other words;
And in this change is my invention spent,
Three themes in one, which wondrous scope affords.   12
    Fair, kind, and true have often lived alone,
      Which three till now never kept seat in one.

4 *one* (in contrast to the 'many' of idolatrous worship); *still* always 6
Still constant always the same 8 *difference* variety 9 *argument* theme
11 *in this change* i.e. in ringing these changes 14 *kept seat* lodged

106

When in the chronicle of wasted time
I see descriptions of the fairest wights,
And beauty making beautiful old rime
4   In praise of ladies dead and lovely knights;
Then, in the blazon of sweet beauty's best,
Of hand, of foot, of lip, of eye, of brow,
I see their antique pen would have expressed
8   Even such a beauty as you master now.
So all their praises are but prophecies
Of this our time, all you prefiguring;
And, for they looked but with divining eyes,
12   They had not skill enough your worth to sing:
        For we, which now behold these present days,
        Have eyes to wonder, but lack tongues to praise.

1 *wasted* past 2 *wights* persons 5 *blazon* commemorative record 8 *master* command 10 *prefiguring* picturing in advance 11 *for* because; *divining* guessing 13 *we* i.e. even we

107

Not mine own fears, nor the prophetic soul
Of the wide world, dreaming on things to come,
Can yet the lease of my true love control,
Supposed as forfeit to a confined doom.   4
The mortal moon hath her eclipse endured,
And the sad augurs mock their own presage;
Incertainties now crown themselves assured,
And peace proclaims olives of endless age.   8
Now with the drops of this most balmy time
My love looks fresh, and Death to me subscribes,
Since, spite of him, I'll live in this poor rime,
While he insults o'er dull and speechless tribes: 12
    And thou in this shalt find thy monument
    When tyrants' crests and tombs of brass are spent.

---

3 *lease* term   **4** *Supposed . . . doom* i.e. presumed to be subject to a limited duration   **5** *mortal . . . endured* (an allusion variously interpreted, most plausibly related to the death in 1603 of Queen Elizabeth, 'Cynthia') **6** *sad augurs* foreboding prognosticators; *presage* predictions   **7** *Incertainties . . . assured* i.e. uncertainty has triumphed as certainty   **8** *olives . . . age* i.e. an eternal continuance of peace   **10** *subscribes* surrenders   **12** *insults* triumphs; *tribes* multitudes   **14** *spent* wasted away

108

What's in the brain that ink may character
Which hath not figured to thee my true spirit?
What's new to speak, what now to register,
4   That may express my love or thy dear merit?
Nothing, sweet boy; but yet, like prayers divine,
I must each day say o'er the very same;
Counting no old thing old, thou mine, I thine,
8   Even as when first I hallowed thy fair name.
So that eternal love in love's fresh case
Weighs not the dust and injury of age,
Nor gives to necessary wrinkles place,
12   But makes antiquity for aye his page,
        Finding the first conceit of love there bred
        Where time and outward form would show it dead.

1 *character* inscribe   2 *figured* revealed   3 *register* record   8 *hallowed* made sacred   9 *fresh case* youthful exterior   10 *Weighs not* cares not for 12 *page* i.e. to wait upon him   13 *conceit* conception

109

O, never say that I was false of heart,
Though absence seemed my flame to qualify;
As easy might I from myself depart
As from my soul, which in thy breast doth lie.   4
That is my home of love: if I have ranged,
Like him that travels I return again,
Just to the time, not with the time exchanged,
So that myself bring water for my stain.   8
Never believe, though in my nature reigned
All frailties that besiege all kinds of blood,
That it could so preposterously be stained
To leave for nothing all thy sum of good;   12
    For nothing this wide universe I call
    Save thou, my rose; in it thou art my all.

2 *qualify* abate, cool   5 *ranged* wandered   7 *Just* punctual; *exchanged*
changed   10 *blood* i.e. flesh   12 *for* in exchange for

110

Alas, 'tis true I have gone here and there
And made myself a motley to the view,
Gored mine own thoughts, sold cheap what is most dear,
4   Made old offenses of affections new.
Most true it is that I have looked on truth
Askance and strangely; but, by all above,
These blenches gave my heart another youth,
8   And worse essays proved thee my best of love.
Now all is done, have what shall have no end:
Mine appetite I never more will grind
On newer proof, to try an older friend,
12   A god in love, to whom I am confined.
     Then give me welcome, next my heaven the best,
     Even to thy pure and most most loving breast.

---

2 *motley* jester   3 *Gored* wounded   4 *offenses* trespasses; *affections* passions   6 *Askance and strangely* i.e. obliquely and at a distance   7 *blenches* turnings aside   8 *worse essays* trials of worse relationships   9 *shall . . . end* i.e. is eternal   10 *grind* whet   11 *proof* test   13 *my heaven* i.e. the Christian heaven

III

O, for my sake do you with Fortune chide,
The guilty goddess of my harmful deeds,
That did not better for my life provide
Than public means which public manners breeds.   4
Thence comes it that my name receives a brand;
And almost thence my nature is subdued
To what it works in, like the dyer's hand:
Pity me then, and wish I were renewed,   8
Whilst, like a willing patient, I will drink
Potions of eisell 'gainst my strong infection;
No bitterness that I will bitter think,
Nor double penance, to correct correction.   12
    Pity me then, dear friend, and I assure ye
    Even that your pity is enough to cure me.

1 *chide* quarrel   2 *guilty goddess* i.e. goddess responsible for   3 *life* liveli-
hood   4 *public means* (probably an allusion to activity in the popular play-
houses)   5 *brand* stigma   6–7 *subdued To* reduced to, made one with
8 *renewed* cleansed   10 *eisell* vinegar (used against the plague)   12 *Nor . . .
correction* i.e. I will not consider the cure worse than the disease

112

Your love and pity doth th' impression fill
Which vulgar scandal stamped upon my brow;
For what care I who calls me well or ill,
4 So you o'ergreen my bad, my good allow?
You are my all the world, and I must strive
To know my shames and praises from your tongue;
None else to me, nor I to none alive,
8 That my steeled sense or changes right or wrong.
In so profound abysm I throw all care
Of others' voices that my adder's sense
To critic and to flatterer stoppèd are;
12 Mark how with my neglect I do dispense:
   You are so strongly in my purpose bred
   That all the world besides methinks are dead.

1 *th' impression fill* i.e. efface the scar 2 *vulgar scandal* i.e. notoriety (as a public performer?) 4 *o'ergreen* conceal with verdure; *allow* approve 6 *shames* faults 7–8 *None . . . wrong* (the sense of this obscure passage seems to be that no other human relationship affects his fixed sense of what is right and wrong) 9 *profound* deep 10 *adder's sense* i.e. deaf ears 12 *how . . . dispense* how I disregard public opinion 13 *so . . . bred* i.e. of such strong influence on my motives

113

Since I left you, mine eye is in my mind,
And that which governs me to go about
Doth part his function and is partly blind,
Seems seeing, but effectually is out;   4
For it no form delivers to the heart
Of bird, of flow'r, or shape which it doth latch;
Of his quick objects hath the mind no part,
Nor his own vision holds what it doth catch;   8
For if it see the rud'st or gentlest sight,
The most sweet favor or deformèd'st creature,
The mountain or the sea, the day or night,
The crow or dove, it shapes them to your feature.   12
    Incapable of more, replete with you,
     My most true mind thus maketh mine eye untrue.

1 *mine . . . mind* i.e. I am directed by inner sight   2 *governs . . . about* i.e. directs my steps   3 *part* divide   3, 7, 8 *his* its (i.e. the physical eye's)   4 *effectually* in effect   6 *latch* catch sight of   7 *quick* fleeting   8 *Nor . . . holds* i.e. nor does the eye itself retain   10 *favor* face   12 *feature* likeness   13 *replete* filled

114

Or whether doth my mind, being crowned with you,
Drink up the monarch's plague, this flattery?
Or whether shall I say mine eye saith true,
4 And that your love taught it this alchemy,
To make of monsters and things indigest
Such cherubins as your sweet self resemble,
Creating every bad a perfect best
8 As fast as objects to his beams assemble?
O, 'tis the first; 'tis flatt'ry in my seeing,
And my great mind most kingly drinks it up:
Mine eye well knows what with his gust is 'greeing,
12 And to his palate doth prepare the cup.
      If it be poisoned, 'tis the lesser sin
      That mine eye loves it and doth first begin.

1, 3 *Or whether* (indicating alternative possibilities) 1 *being . . . you* i.e.
by being crowned by you 4 *alchemy* i.e. power to transform substances
5 *indigest* shapeless 6 *cherubins* angelic forms 8 *to . . . assemble* i.e. are
presented to the eye's gaze 11 *with . . . 'greeing* is agreeable to the mind's
taste 14 *That* since

115

Those lines that I before have writ do lie,
Even those that said I could not love you dearer;
Yet then my judgment knew no reason why
My most full flame should afterwards burn clearer.   4
But reckoning Time, whose millioned accidents
Creep in 'twixt vows and change decrees of kings,
Tan sacred beauty, blunt the sharp'st intents,
Divert strong minds to th' course of alt'ring things!   8
Alas, why, fearing of Time's tyranny,
Might I not then say, 'Now I love you best'
When I was certain o'er incertainty,
Crowning the present, doubting of the rest?   12
    Love is a babe; then might I not say so,
    To give full growth to that which still doth grow.

---

2 *dearer* more dearly   **5** *reckoning . . . accidents* i.e. time whose casual events are reckoned in the millions   **7** *Tan* coarsen; *intents* intentions   **8** *Divert* accommodate; *alt'ring things* things as they change   **12** *Crowning* glorifying   **13** *then* therefore; *so* i.e. 'Now I love you best'

116

Let me not to the marriage of true minds
Admit impediments; love is not love
Which alters when it alteration finds
4   Or bends with the remover to remove.
O, no, it is an ever-fixèd mark
That looks on tempests and is never shaken;
It is the star to every wand'ring bark,
8   Whose worth's unknown, although his height be taken.
Love's not Time's fool, though rosy lips and cheeks
Within his bending sickle's compass come;
Love alters not with his brief hours and weeks,
12   But bears it out even to the edge of doom.
    If this be error, and upon me proved,
    I never writ, nor no man ever loved.

2 *impediments* (an echo of the marriage service)   4 *bends . . . remove* i.e. agrees with the withdrawer to withdraw   5 *mark* sea-mark   8 *worth 's unknown* i.e. value is incalculable; *his height* the star's altitude   9 *fool* plaything   10 *Within . . . compass* i.e. within the range of Time's curving sickle   11 *his* Time's   12 *bears it out* persists   13 *upon* against

117

Accuse me thus, that I have scanted all
Wherein I should your great deserts repay;
Forgot upon your dearest love to call,
Whereto all bonds do tie me day by day;   4
That I have frequent been with unknown minds
And given to time your own dear-purchased right;
That I have hoisted sail to all the winds
Which should transport me farthest from your sight.   8
Book both my wilfulness and errors down,
And on just proof surmise accumulate;
Bring me within the level of your frown,
But shoot not at me in your wakened hate: 12
    Since my appeal says I did strive to prove
    The constancy and virtue of your love.

---

1 *scanted* come short of   **3** *Forgot . . . call* have forgotten to invoke your most precious love   **4** *bonds* obligations   **5** *frequent* familiar; *unknown minds* i.e. negligible spirits   **6** *given to time* i.e. wasted away   **9** *Book . . . down* i.e. record both my intentional and unintentional trespasses   **10** *on . . . accumulate* i.e. take account of valid circumstantial evidence   **11** *level* range   **13** *appeal* plea; *strive to prove* i.e. thus try to test

118

Like as to make our appetites more keen,
With eager compounds we our palate urge;
As to prevent our maladies unseen,
4   We sicken to shun sickness when we purge:
Even so, being full of your ne'er-cloying sweetness,
To bitter sauces did I frame my feeding;
And, sick of welfare, found a kind of meetness
8   To be diseased ere that there was true needing.
Thus policy in love, t' anticipate
The ills that were not, grew to faults assured,
And brought to medicine a healthful state
12   Which, rank of goodness, would by ill be cured.
       But thence I learn, and find the lesson true,
       Drugs poison him that so fell sick of you.

1 *Like as* just as   2 *eager compounds* sharp condiments; *urge* stimulate
3 *As* just as; *prevent* ward off, forestall   6 *bitter sauces* i.e. unsavory per-
sons; *frame* direct   7 *meetness* appropriateness   9 *anticipate* forestall   10
faults assured actual faults   11 *medicine* i.e. medical treatment   12 *rank*
too full   14 *so* thus

119

What potions have I drunk of Siren tears
Distilled from limbecks foul as hell within,
Applying fears to hopes and hopes to fears,
Still losing when I saw myself to win!   4
What wretched errors hath my heart committed
Whilst it hath thought itself so blessèd never!
How have mine eyes out of their spheres been fitted
In the distraction of this madding fever!   8
O benefit of ill; now I find true
That better is by evil still made better;
And ruined love, when it is built anew,
Grows fairer than at first, more strong, far greater.   12
    So I return rebuked to my content,
    And gain by ills thrice more than I have spent.

1 *Siren tears* i.e. appeals of the temptress   2 *limbecks* alembics, stills (i.e. the person of the temptress)   3 *Applying* i.e. as a salve   4 *Still* always; *saw myself* expected   6 *so blessèd never* never so blessed   7 *spheres* sockets (?), orbits (?); *fitted* forced by fits   8 *madding* maddening, producing delirium

120

That you were once unkind befriends me now,
And for that sorrow which I then did feel
Needs must I under my transgression bow,
4 Unless my nerves were brass or hammered steel.
For if you were by my unkindness shaken,
As I by yours, you've passed a hell of time,
And I, a tyrant, have no leisure taken
8 To weigh how once I suffered in your crime.
O that our night of woe might have rememb'red
My deepest sense how hard true sorrow hits,
And soon to you, as you to me then, tend'red
12 The humble salve which wounded bosoms fits!
    But that your trespass now becomes a fee;
    Mine ransoms yours, and yours must ransom me.

2 *for* because of   3 *my transgression* i.e. my present unkindness to you
4 *nerves* sinews   7 *tyrant* oppressor; *no leisure taken* i.e. failed to take the
time   8 *weigh* consider; *crime* i.e. unkindness to me   9 *night of woe* i.e.
estrangement, for which you were responsible; *rememb'red* reminded
11 *tend'red* offered   12 *salve* apology; *fits* suits   13 *fee* payment   14
ransoms redeems, excuses

121

'Tis better to be vile than vile esteemed
When not to be receives reproach of being,
And the just pleasure lost, which is so deemed
Not by our feeling but by others' seeing.   4
For why should others' false adulterate eyes
Give salutation to my sportive blood?
Or on my frailties why are frailer spies,
Which in their wills count bad what I think good?   8
No, I am that I am; and they that level
At my abuses reckon up their own:
I may be straight though they themselves be bevel;
By their rank thoughts my deeds must not be shown, 12
    Unless this general evil they maintain:
    All men are bad and in their badness reign.

1 *esteemed* considered   2 *not to be* i.e. not to be vile; *being* i.e. being vile 3 *just* right, proper; *so* i.e. vile   4 *Not . . . seeing* i.e. not in our own mind but in the view of others   5 *false adulterate* prurient   6 *Give salutation to* greet, i.e. meet more than halfway; *sportive* wanton   7 *frailties* faults; *frailer* faultier   8 *in their wills* i.e. wishfully   9 *that* what; *level* aim   10 *abuses* transgressions   11 *bevel* i.e. crooked

122

Thy gift, thy tables, are within my brain
Full charactered with lasting memory,
Which shall above that idle rank remain
4   Beyond all date, even to eternity;
Or, at the least, so long as brain and heart
Have faculty by nature to subsist,
Till each to rased oblivion yield his part
8   Of thee, thy record never can be missed.
That poor retention could not so much hold,
Nor need I tallies thy dear love to score;
Therefore to give them from me was I bold,
12   To trust those tables that receive thee more.
      To keep an adjunct to remember thee
      Were to import forgetfulness in me.

1 *tables* writing-tablet   **2** *charactered* inscribed   **3** *that idle rank* the leaves of the tablet (?); *remain* endure   **6** *faculty . . . subsist* natural power to survive   **7** *rased* blank; *his* its   **8** *missed* lost   **9** *retention* retainer (i.e. the tablet)   **10** *tallies* anything on which scores were kept   **11** *to . . . from me* i.e. to give away that tablet   **12** *those tables* i.e. the tablet of the memory   **13** *adjunct* aid, implement   **14** *import* imply

123

No, Time, thou shalt not boast that I do change:
Thy pyramids built up with newer might
To me are nothing novel, nothing strange;
They are but dressings of a former sight.   **4**
Our dates are brief, and therefore we admire
What thou dost foist upon us that is old,
And rather make them born to our desire
Than think that we before have heard them told.   **8**
Thy registers and thee I both defy,
Not wond'ring at the present nor the past;
For thy records and what we see doth lie,
Made more or less by thy continual haste.   **12**
    This I do vow, and this shall ever be:
    I will be true, despite thy scythe and thee.

2 *pyramids . . . might* (perhaps a topical allusion, possibly to the pyramids erected on London streets as part of the pageant welcoming King James in 1603; cf. Sonnet 107)   4 *dressings* i.e. imitations   5 *dates* life-spans   7 *born . . . desire* i.e. created newly to our taste   8 *told* reckoned   9 *registers* records of time   11 *records . . . see* i.e. both past and present; *lie* mis-represent

124

If my dear love were but the child of state,
It might for Fortune's bastard be unfathered,
As subject to Time's love or to Time's hate,
4   Weeds among weeds, or flowers with flowers gathered.
No, it was builded far from accident;
It suffers not in smiling pomp, nor falls
Under the blow of thrallèd discontent,
8   Whereto th' inviting time our fashion calls:
It fears not Policy, that heretic
Which works on leases of short-numb'red hours,
But all alone stands hugely politic,
12   That it nor grows with heat nor drowns with show'rs.
      To this I witness call the fools of Time,
      Which die for goodness, who have lived for crime.

---

1 *love* love of you; *but* only; *child of state* i.e. product of material circum-
stances   2 *for . . . unfathered* i.e. go unclaimed, as Fortune's bastard   5
accident chance occurrence   7 *thrallèd* oppressed   8 *Whereto . . . calls* to
which condition our times invite us (?)   9 *Policy, that heretic* i.e. false
practicality   10 *on . . . hours* i.e. on short-term leases   11 *all . . . politic* i.e.
only love is truly practical   12 *That it nor* since it neither   13 *fools* play-
things   14 *Which . . . crime* i.e. eleventh-hour repenters (often dubiously
associated with various Catholic or other martyrs of the time)

125

Were't aught to me I bore the canopy,
With my extern the outward honoring,
Or laid great bases for eternity,
Which proves more short than waste or ruining?   4
Have I not seen dwellers on form and favor
Lose all and more by paying too much rent,
For compound sweet forgoing simple savor,
Pitiful thrivers, in their gazing spent?   8
No, let me be obsequious in thy heart,
And take thou my oblation, poor but free,
Which is not mixed with seconds, knows no art
But mutual render, only me for thee.   12
    Hence, thou suborned informer; a true soul
    When most impeached stands least in thy control.

1 *Were't aught* would it be anything; *canopy* i.e. the covering with which the persons of the great are honored   2 *With . . . honoring* i.e. externally honoring the external   3 *bases* foundations (of monuments)   5 *dwellers on* i.e. those who dwell upon or overvalue (with pun on 'tenants')   8 *Pitiful thrivers* i.e. those who thrive pitifully since their gains are empty; *in . . . spent* i.e. starved by mere looking   9 *be obsequious* have my devotion recognized   10 *oblation* offering   11 *seconds* i.e. second-best, inferior; *art* artifice   12 *mutual . . . thee* i.e. surrender of my true self for your true self   13 *suborned informer* false witness   14 *impeached* accused

126

O thou, my lovely boy, who in thy power
Dost hold Time's fickle glass, his sickle hour;
Who hast by waning grown, and therein show'st
4   Thy lovers withering as thy sweet self grow'st;
If Nature, sovereign mistress over wrack,
As thou goest onwards, still will pluck thee back,
She keeps thee to this purpose, that her skill
8   May Time disgrace and wretched minutes kill.
Yet fear her, O thou minion of her pleasure!
She may detain, but not still keep, her treasure;
Her audit, though delayed, answered must be,
12   And her quietus is to render thee.

2 *glass* mirror; *hour* hourglass   3 *by waning grown* i.e. increased in love-liness with the passing of time; *show'st* i.e. show in contrast   5 *wrack* wreckage, ruin   9 *minion* darling   11 *audit* final reckoning; *answered* paid   12 *quietus* settlement; *render* surrender

Number 126 is exceptional among the sonnets, since it is a poem of twelve lines rhyming in pairs.

127

In the old age black was not counted fair,
Or, if it were, it bore not beauty's name;
But now is black beauty's successive heir,
And beauty slandered with a bastard shame;   4
For since each hand hath put on nature's power,
Fairing the foul with art's false borrowed face,
Sweet beauty hath no name, no holy bower,
But is profaned, if not lives in disgrace.   8
Therefore my mistress' brows are raven black,
Her eyes so suited, and they mourners seem
At such who, not born fair, no beauty lack,
Sland'ring creation with a false esteem: 12
　　Yet so they mourn, becoming of their woe,
　　That every tongue says beauty should look so.

1 *old* former; *black* i.e. brunette (equated with ugliness); *fair* beautiful
(with play on 'blonde') 3 *successive heir* heir in line of succession 4
slandered . . . shame i.e. declared illegitimate 5 *put* taken 6 *Fairing*
beautifying; *art's . . . face* i.e. cosmetics 7 *Sweet beauty* i.e. natural blonde
beauty; *holy bower* i.e. shrine 8 *if . . . disgrace* (the sense seems to be that
blonde beauty is so habitually enhanced or simulated with cosmetics that it
is discredited in its natural form) 10 *so suited* i.e. also black 11 *At* for;
no beauty lack i.e. nevertheless possess the appearance of beauty 12
Sland'ring . . . esteem i.e. misrepresenting the natural process with counter-
feit value 13 *becoming of* gracing

128

How oft, when thou, my music, music play'st
Upon that blessèd wood whose motion sounds
With thy sweet fingers when thou gently sway'st
4   The wiry concord that mine ear confounds,
Do I envy those jacks that nimble leap
To kiss the tender inward of thy hand,
Whilst my poor lips, which should that harvest reap,
8   At the wood's boldness by thee blushing stand.
To be so tickled they would change their state
And situation with those dancing chips
O'er whom thy fingers walk with gentle gait,
12   Making dead wood more blest than living lips.
        Since saucy jacks so happy are in this,
        Give them thy fingers, me thy lips to kiss.

2 *wood* keys of the spinet or virginal; *motion* mechanism   3 *thou* . . .
sway'st you . . . control   4 *wiry concord* harmony of strings; *confounds* i.e.
makes swoon   5 *jacks* (not the keys proper, which would be touched by the
finger-tips, but the levers which on some virginals touched the *tender
inward* of the hand when the instrument was played or tuned)   9 *they* i.e.
the lips

129

Th' expense of spirit in a waste of shame
Is lust in action; and, till action, lust
Is perjured, murd'rous, bloody, full of blame,
Savage, extreme, rude, cruel, not to trust;   4
Enjoyed no sooner but despisèd straight;
Past reason hunted, and no sooner had,
Past reason hated as a swallowed bait
On purpose laid to make the taker mad: 8
Mad in pursuit, and in possession so;
Had, having, and in quest to have, extreme;
A bliss in proof, and proved, a very woe;
Before, a joy proposed; behind, a dream.   12
    All this the world well knows; yet none knows well
    To shun the heaven that leads men to this hell.

---

1 *Th' expense . . . shame* i.e. the expenditure of vital power in shameful waste
2 *action* consummation   4 *rude* brutal; *to trust* to be trusted   6 *Past
reason hunted* i.e. madly sought   10 *quest* pursuit; *extreme* excessive, given
to extremes   11 *in proof* in testing; *proved* tested   12 *dream* delusion   14
heaven i.e. promise of bliss

130

My mistress' eyes are nothing like the sun;
Coral is far more red than her lips' red;
If snow be white, why then her breasts are dun;
4   If hairs be wires, black wires grow on her head.
I have seen roses damasked, red and white,
But no such roses see I in her cheeks;
And in some perfumes is there more delight
8   Than in the breath that from my mistress reeks.
I love to hear her speak; yet well I know
That music hath a far more pleasing sound:
I grant I never saw a goddess go;
12   My mistress, when she walks, treads on the ground.
    And yet, by heaven, I think my love as rare
    As any she belied with false compare.

5 *damasked* mingled red and white **8** *reeks* breathes forth **11** *go* walk
14 *compare* comparison (with sun, coral, snow, etc.)

131

Thou art as tyrannous, so as thou art,
As those whose beauties proudly make them cruel;
For well thou know'st to my dear, doting heart
Thou art the fairest and most precious jewel.　　　　4
Yet, in good faith, some say that thee behold,
Thy face hath not the power to make love groan;
To say they err I dare not be so bold,
Although I swear it to myself alone.　　　　8
And, to be sure that is not false I swear,
A thousand groans, but thinking on thy face,
One on another's neck, do witness bear
Thy black is fairest in my judgment's place.　　　　12
　　In nothing art thou black save in thy deeds,
　　And thence this slander, as I think, proceeds.

1 *so . . . art* even as you are (i.e. not a recognized beauty)　3 *dear* fond　8 *Although* (1) even providing that, (2) however (humorously ambiguous: it is not made certain whether the poet does or does not agree privately with her critics)　9 *to be sure* i.e. for proof　10 *but thinking* when I only think of　11 *One . . . neck* i.e. in quick succession　12 *in . . . place* where my judgment is　13 *black* i.e. not fair, foul

132

Thine eyes I love, and they, as pitying me,
Knowing thy heart torments me with disdain,
Have put on black and loving mourners be,
4   Looking with pretty ruth upon my pain.
And truly not the morning sun of heaven
Better becomes the gray cheeks of the east,
Nor that full star that ushers in the even
8   Doth half that glory to the sober west,
As those two mourning eyes become thy face.
O, let it then as well beseem thy heart
To mourn for me, since mourning doth thee grace,
12   And suit thy pity like in every part.
    Then will I swear beauty herself is black,
    And all they foul that thy complexion lack.

4 *ruth* pity   6 *becomes . . . cheeks* i.e. adorns the early-morning sky   7 *even* evening 8 *Doth* i.e. renders 9 *mourning* (1) mourning, (2) morning 10 *beseem* i.e. be seemly to 12 *suit . . . like* dress your pity alike; *every part* i.e. *heart* as well as *eyes*

133

Beshrew that heart that makes my heart to groan
For that deep wound it gives my friend and me:
Is't not enough to torture me alone,
But slave to slavery my sweet'st friend must be?　　4
Me from myself thy cruel eye hath taken,
And my next self thou harder hast engrossed;
Of him, myself, and thee I am forsaken,
A torment thrice threefold thus to be crossed.　　8
Prison my heart in thy steel bosom's ward,
But then my friend's heart let my poor heart bail;
Whoe'er keeps me, let my heart be his guard:
Thou canst not then use rigor in my jail.　　12
　　And yet thou wilt; for I, being pent in thee,
　　Perforce am thine, and all that is in me.

1 *Beshrew* curse (mild in connotation)　2 *For* because of　4 *slave to slavery* i.e. sharer of my enslavement　5 *myself* i.e. my true self　6 *my . . . engrossed* i.e. you have placed my friend under even greater bondage　8 *crossed* afflicted　9 *ward* bondage　10 *bail* i.e. free by serving as substitute　11 *keeps* imprisons; *his guard* my friend's guardhouse　12 *rigor* cruelty; *jail* i.e. heart which holds the friend　13 *pent* pent up

134

So, now I have confessed that he is thine
And I myself am mortgaged to thy will,
Myself I'll forfeit, so that other mine
4   Thou wilt restore to be my comfort still:
But thou wilt not, nor he will not be free,
For thou art covetous, and he is kind;
He learned but surety-like to write for me
8   Under that bond that him as fast doth bind.
The statute of thy beauty thou wilt take,
Thou usurer that put'st forth all to use,
And sue a friend came debtor for my sake;
12   So him I lose through my unkind abuse.
    Him have I lost, thou hast both him and me;
    He pays the whole, and yet am I not free.

---

2 *mortgaged* held as security; *will* (1) purpose, (2) carnal desire   3 *other mine* i.e. alter ego   4 *restore* return; *still* always, in the future   5 *will not* (1) will not, (2) wills not to   6 *kind* compliant   7–8 *He . . . bind* i.e. it was as if to serve as security for me that he signed the bond that now binds us both (with a play on *learned . . . to write for me* in the sense of 'took my place with my mistress')   9 *take* invoke   10 *use* usury   11 *came* who became 12 *my unkind abuse* i.e. your deceiving me

135

Whoever hath her wish, thou hast thy Will,
And Will to boot, and Will in overplus.
More than enough am I that vex thee still,
To thy sweet will making addition thus.   4
Wilt thou, whose will is large and spacious,
Not once vouchsafe to hide my will in thine?
Shall will in others seem right gracious,
And in my will no fair acceptance shine?   8
The sea, all water, yet receives rain still
And in abundance addeth to his store;
So thou, being rich in Will, add to thy Will
One will of mine to make thy large Will more.   12
    Let no unkind, no fair beseechers kill;
    Think all but one, and me in that one Will.

1 *Will* (1) one of various persons named 'Will,' including the poet and perhaps the friend and the husband, (2) carnal desire ('Will' is both capitalized and italicized in Q wherever capitalized here, in the present sonnet and Sonnet 136)   **2** *to boot* i.e. in addition   **3** *still* always   **4** *will* (where so printed, here and in Q, the word seems usually to have the more neutral meaning of 'wish,' but it incorporates an indeterminable number of puns); *making addition thus* i.e. by adding myself   **6** *vouchsafe* consent; *hide* shelter   **8** *acceptance* acceptability   **10** *his* its   **13** *no unkind* i.e. no unkind word, no refusal; *no fair beseechers* i.e. no applicants for your favors (as punctuated, here and in Q, the line contains a double negative; some editors omit the comma and place the 'no' in quotation marks)   **14** *and me* i.e. including me

136

If thy soul check thee that I come so near,
Swear to thy blind soul that I was thy Will,
And will, thy soul knows, is admitted there:
4 Thus far for love my love-suit, sweet, fulfil.
Will will fulfil the treasure of thy love
Ay, fill it full with wills, and my will one.
In things of great receipt with ease we prove
8 Among a number one is reckoned none.
Then in the number let me pass untold,
Though in thy store's account I one must be;
For nothing hold me, so it please thee hold
12 That nothing me, a something, sweet, to thee.
   Make but my name thy love, and love that still,
   And then thou lovest me, for my name is Will.

1 *check* rebuke; *come so near* (1) am so candid, (2) have access to you **2** *blind* obtuse **4** *fulfil* grant **5** *fulfil the treasure* fill the treasury **6** *one* among them **7** *receipt* capacity **8** *reckoned none* not counted (cf. an adage of the time, 'one is no number') **9** *untold* uncounted **10** *thy store's account* i.e. the inventory of your numerous lovers **13** *my name* i.e. 'will,' in the sense of 'carnal desire'

137

Thou blind fool, Love, what dost thou to mine eyes
 That they behold and see not what they see?
They know what beauty is, see where it lies,
Yet what the best is take the worst to be.   4
If eyes, corrupt by over-partial looks,
Be anchored in the bay where all men ride,
Why of eyes' falsehood hast thou forgèd hooks,
Whereto the judgment of my heart is tied?   8
Why should my heart think that a several plot
Which my heart knows the wide world's common place?
Or mine eyes seeing this, say this is not,
To put fair truth upon so foul a face?   12
    In things right true my heart and eyes have erred,
    And to this false plague are they now transferred.

3 *lies* resides   5 *corrupt* corrupted   6 *Be . . . ride* i.e. have brought me to anchor in a common roadway (with *double entendre* in 'ride')   7 *false-hood* deception; *forgèd* fashioned   9 *that . . . plot* i.e. that plot a private one   10 *knows* knows to be   11 *not* not so   13 *erred* gone astray   14 *false plague* (1) plague of falseness, (2) plaguey mistress

138

When my love swears that she is made of truth
I do believe her, though I know she lies,
That she might think me some untutored youth,
Unlearnèd in the world's false subtilties.
Thus vainly thinking that she thinks me young,
Although she knows my days are past the best,
Simply I credit her false-speaking tongue;
On both sides thus is simple truth suppressed.
But wherefore says she not she is unjust?
And wherefore say not I that I am old?
O, love's best habit is in seeming trust,
And age in love loves not to have years told.
        Therefore I lie with her and she with me,
        And in our faults by lies we flattered be.

---

1 *truth* fidelity   **2** *believe* seem to believe   **5** *vainly thinking* i.e. acting as if I thought   **7** *Simply* pretending to be simple; *credit* give credence to   **9** *unjust* unfaithful   **11** *habit* dress, guise; *seeming trust* apparent fidelity   **12** *told* counted   **13** *lie with* i.e. lie to (with *double entendre*)

In the version of the above sonnet printed in *The Passionate Pilgrim* (1st ed. 1599) the following variants appear: **4** *Unlearnèd* Unskillful *subtilties* forgeries   **6** *she knows my days are* I know my years be   **7** *Simply I* I smiling   **8** *On both sides thus is simple truth suppressed* Outfacing faults in love, with love's ill rest   **9** *she not she is unjust* my love that she is young   **11** *habit is in seeming trust* habit's in a soothing tongue   **12** *t'* to (the reading here adopted)   **13** *I . . . her . . . she* I'll . . . love . . . love   **14** *And in our faults by lies we flattered be* Since that our faults in love thus smothered be

139

O, call not me to justify the wrong
That thy unkindness lays upon my heart;
Wound me not with thine eye but with thy tongue;
Use power with power, and slay me not by art.   4

Tell me thou lov'st elsewhere; but in my sight,
Dear heart, forbear to glance thine eye aside;
What need'st thou wound with cunning when thy might
Is more than my o'erpressed defense can bide?   8

Let me excuse thee: ah, my love well knows
Her pretty looks have been mine enemies;
And therefore from my face she turns my foes,
That they elsewhere might dart their injuries: 2

    Yet do not so; but since I am near slain,
    Kill me outright with looks and rid my pain.

1 *call* call on, ask   2 *unkindness* i.e. infidelity   3 *not . . . tongue* i.e. not with roving looks but with actual words   4 *Use . . . power* i.e. use your power directly; *art* artifice   5 *but* while   8 *o'erpressed* i.e. attacked beyond its power to withstand; *bide* stand   9 *excuse thee* i.e. excuse you thus   11 *foes* i.e. the *pretty looks*   14 *rid* dispatch

140

Be wise as thou art cruel: do not press
My tongue-tied patience with too much disdain,
Lest sorrow lend me words, and words express
4   The manner of my pity-wanting pain.
If I might teach thee wit, better it were,
Though not to love, yet, love, to tell me so;
As testy sick men, when their deaths be near,
8   No news but health from their physicians know.
For if I should despair, I should grow mad,
And in my madness might speak ill of thee:
Now this ill-wresting world is grown so bad
12   Mad slanderers by mad ears believèd be.
    That I may not be so, nor thou belied,
    Bear thine eyes straight, though thy proud heart go wide.

1 *press* oppress   4 *manner* nature; *pity-wanting* unpitied   5 *wit* wisdom
6 *so* i.e. that you do love me   7 *testy* peevish   8 *know* i.e. hear   11 *ill-wresting* i.e. that wrests things to an evil sense   13 *so* i.e. a 'mad slanderer'
14 *wide* astray

141

In faith, I do not love thee with mine eyes,
For they in thee a thousand errors note;
But 'tis my heart that loves what they despise,
Who in despite of view is pleased to dote.   4
Nor are mine ears with thy tongue's tune delighted,
Nor tender feeling to base touches prone,
Nor taste, nor smell, desire to be invited
To any sensual feast with thee alone;   8
But my five wits nor my five senses can
Dissuade one foolish heart from serving thee,
Who leaves unswayed the likeness of a man,
Thy proud heart's slave and vassal wretch to be: 12
    Only my plague thus far I count my gain,
    That she that makes me sin awards me pain.

4 *Who ... view* i.e. which in spite of what is seen   6 *Nor ... prone* i.e. nor does the delicate sense of feeling incline toward contact with you   8 *sensual feast* feast of the senses   9 *But* but neither; *five wits* (the mental faculties, such as intelligence, imagination, memory, etc.)   11 *Who ... man* i.e. which leaves ungoverned the outer man (i.e. the heart, which should be monarch of the body, has abdicated to become another's heart's slave)   13 *Only ... gain* i.e. one thing certain, my suffering is to my advantage to the following extent   14 *That ... pain* i.e. the sin is its own punishment

142

Love is my sin, and thy dear virtue hate,
Hate of my sin, grounded on sinful loving.
O, but with mine compare thou thine own state,
4 And thou shalt find it merits not reproving;
Or if it do, not from those lips of thine,
That have profaned their scarlet ornaments
And sealed false bonds of love as oft as mine,
8 Robbed others' beds' revenues of their rents.
Be it lawful I love thee as thou lov'st those
Whom thine eyes woo as mine importune thee:
Root pity in thy heart, that, when it grows,
12 Thy pity may deserve to pitied be.
      If thou dost seek to have what thou dost hide,
      By self-example mayst thou be denied.

2 *Hate . . . loving* i.e. hate of the adulterous character of my love   4 *it* i.e. my state   6 *scarlet ornaments* i.e. the lips (here equated with the seals of red wax authenticating documents)   7 *mine* i.e. mine have   8 *Robbed . . . rents* i.e. and stolen from wives the due of the marriage bed   9 *Be it lawful* i.e. consider it lawful that   12 *Thy . . . be* i.e. your pity will make you deserving of pity   13 *hide* withhold

143

Lo, as a careful housewife runs to catch
One of her feathered creatures broke away,
Sets down her babe, and makes all swift dispatch
In pursuit of the thing she would have stay;   4
Whilst her neglected child holds her in chase,
Cries to catch her whose busy care is bent
To follow that which flies before her face,
Not prizing her poor infant's discontent: 8
So runn'st thou after that which flies from thee,
Whilst I, thy babe, chase thee afar behind;
But if thou catch thy hope, turn back to me
And play the mother's part, kiss me, be kind.   12
  So will I pray that thou mayst have thy Will,
  If thou turn back and my loud crying still.

3 *dispatch* haste 5 *holds . . . chase* i.e. chases her in turn 8 *prizing* considering important 11 *hope* hoped-for object 13 *Will* (capitalized and italicized in Q; cf. Sonnets 135 and 136)

144

Two loves I have, of comfort and despair,
Which like two spirits do suggest me still:
The better angel is a man right fair,
4   The worser spirit a woman colored ill.
To win me soon to hell, my female evil
Tempteth my better angel from my side,
And would corrupt my saint to be a devil,
8   Wooing his purity with her foul pride.
And whether that my angel be turned fiend
Suspect I may, yet not directly tell;
But being both from me, both to each friend,
12   I guess one angel in another's hell.
    Yet this shall I ne'er know, but live in doubt,
    Till my bad angel fire my good one out.

1 *comfort and despair* i.e. mercy and despair (in Christian theology in-strumental respectively in bringing the soul to salvation and damnation) 2 *suggest me still* always prompt me   4 *colored ill* i.e. dark   5 *evil* evil angel 8 *pride* sexual heat   11 *each* each other   12 *in another's hell* (a *double entendre*)   14 *fire . . . out* i.e. infect with venereal disease

In the version of the above sonnet printed in *The Passionate Pilgrim* (1st ed. 1599) the following variants appear: 2 *Which* That   3 *The* My   4 *The* My   6 *sight* side (the reading here adopted)   8 *foul* fair   9 *find* fiend (the reading here adopted)   11 *But . . . from* For . . . to   13 *Yet this shall I ne'er* The truth I shall not

145

Those lips that Love's own hand did make
Breathed forth the sound that said 'I hate'
To me that languished for her sake;
But when she saw my woeful state,   4
Straight in her heart did mercy come,
Chiding that tongue that ever sweet
Was used in giving gentle doom,
And taught it thus anew to greet: 8
'I hate' she altered with an end
That followed it as gentle day
Doth follow night, who, like a fiend,
From heaven to hell is flown away.   12
    'I hate' from hate away she threw,
    And saved my life, saying 'not you.'

7 *doom* sentence, judgment   8 *greet* i.e. accost me

The authenticity of this sonnet, in tetrameters and rudimentary diction, has been questioned, with considerable show of reason; in any case, it is not in context with the adjacent sonnets.

146

Poor soul, the center of my sinful earth,
[Fooled by] these rebel pow'rs that thee array,
Why dost thou pine within and suffer dearth,
4   Painting thy outward walls so costly gay?
Why so large cost, having so short a lease,
Dost thou upon thy fading mansion spend?
Shall worms, inheritors of this excess,
8   Eat up thy charge? Is this thy body's end?
Then, soul, live thou upon thy servant's loss,
And let that pine to aggravate thy store;
Buy terms divine in selling hours of dross;
12   Within be fed, without be rich no more:
      So shalt thou feed on Death, that feeds on men,
      And Death once dead, there's no more dying then.

1 *earth* i.e. body   2 *Fooled by* (Malone's conjecture; Q repeats 'My sinful earth'); *rebel pow'rs* rebellious flesh; *array* dress, enclose   4 *Painting* i.e. while ornamenting   5 *cost* sums   8 *charge* i.e. the costly body   9 *servant's* body's   10 *aggravate* increase   11 *terms divine* immortality in heaven; *hours of dross* wasteful hours

147

My love is as a fever, longing still
For that which longer nurseth the disease,
Feeding on that which doth preserve the ill,
Th' uncertain sickly appetite to please.   4
My reason, the physician to my love,
Angry that his prescriptions are not kept,
Hath left me, and I desperate now approve
Desire is death, which physic did except.   8
Past cure I am, now reason is past care,
And frantic-mad with evermore unrest;
My thoughts and my discourse as madmen's are,
At randon from the truth vainly expressed: 12
    For I have sworn thee fair, and thought thee bright,
    Who art as black as hell, as dark as night.

1 *still* always   2 *longer nurseth* prolongs   4 *uncertain* fickle   6 *kept* followed   7 *approve* i.e. prove by my experience that   8 *Desire . . . except* i.e. desire, which rejected reason's medicine, proves fatal   12 *At randon* at random, in deviation

148

O me, what eyes hath Love put in my head,
Which have no correspondence with true sight;
Or, if they have, where is my judgment fled,
4   That censures falsely what they see aright?
If that be fair whereon my false eyes dote,
What means the world to say it is not so?
If it be not, then love doth well denote
8   Love's eye is not so true as all men's no.
How can it? O, how can Love's eye be true,
That is so vexed with watching and with tears?
No marvel then though I mistake my view:
12   The sun itself sees not till heaven clears.
    O cunning Love, with tears thou keep'st me blind,
    Lest eyes well-seeing thy foul faults should find.

4 *censures* judges   7 *denote* indicate   8 *Love's eye* i.e. Love's 'ay' (punning
with *men's no*)   10 *vexed* afflicted; *watching* lying awake   11 *my view* i.e.
what I see   14 *find* discover

149

Canst thou, O cruel, say I love thee not
When I against myself with thee partake?
Do I not think on thee when I forgot
Am of myself, all tyrant for thy sake?   4
Who hateth thee that I do call my friend?
On whom frown'st thou that I do fawn upon?
Nay, if thou lour'st on me, do I not spend
Revenge upon myself with present moan?   8
What merit do I in myself respect
That is so proud thy service to despise,
When all my best doth worship thy defect,
Commanded by the motion of thine eyes?   12

    But, love, hate on, for now I know thy mind;
    Those that can see thou lov'st, and I am blind.

2 *partake* join   **3–4** *I forgot . . . myself* i.e. I forget myself   **4** *all tyrant* complete self-oppressor   **7** *thou lour'st* you frown   **8** *present moan* immediate suffering   **10** *thy . . . despise* i.e. as to despise serving you   **11** *defect* insufficiency (cf. Sonnet 150, l. 2)   **14** *Those . . . lov'st* i.e. you love those who can see

150

O, from what pow'r hast thou this pow'rful might
With insufficiency my heart to sway?
To make me give the lie to my true sight
4   And swear that brightness doth not grace the day?
Whence hast thou this becoming of things ill,
That in the very refuse of thy deeds
There is such strength and warrantise of skill
8   That in my mind thy worst all best exceeds?
Who taught thee how to make me love thee more,
The more I hear and see just cause of hate?
O, though I love what others do abhor,
12   With others thou shouldst not abhor my state:
      If thy unworthiness raised love in me,
      More worthy I to be beloved of thee.

2 *sway* rule   **4** *that . . . day* (the opposite, that darkness graces the day, is implied)   **5** *becoming . . . ill* i.e. power to lend grace to evil things   **6** *very . . . deeds* most worthless of your actions   **7** *warrantise of skill* warranty of competence   **12** *state* i.e. bemused condition

151

Love is too young to know what conscience is;
Yet who knows not conscience is born of love?
Then, gentle cheater, urge not my amiss,
Lest guilty of my faults thy sweet self prove.   4
For, thou betraying me, I do betray
My nobler part to my gross body's treason;
My soul doth tell my body that he may
Triumph in love; flesh stays no farther reason,   8
But, rising at thy name, doth point out thee
As his triumphant prize. Proud of this pride,
He is contented thy poor drudge to be,
To stand in thy affairs, fall by thy side.   12
    No want of conscience hold it that I call
    Her 'love' for whose dear love I rise and fall.

1 *conscience* consciousness, awareness   3 *cheater* betrayer; *urge . . . amiss* i.e. do not press charges against me   8 *stays* awaits; *reason* reasoning   9 *rising* revolting (with *double entendre*)   10 *pride* i.e. heat   13 *want of conscience* lack of awareness

152

In loving thee thou know'st I am forsworn,
But thou art twice forsworn, to me love swearing;
In act thy bed-vow broke, and new faith torn
In vowing new hate after new love bearing.
But why of two oaths' breach do I accuse thee
When I break twenty? I am perjured most,
For all my vows are oaths but to misuse thee,
And all my honest faith in thee is lost;
For I have sworn deep oaths of thy deep kindness,
Oaths of thy love, thy truth, thy constancy;
And, to enlighten thee, gave eyes to blindness,
Or made them swear against the thing they see;
    For I have sworn thee fair: more perjured eye,
    To swear against the truth so foul a lie.

4

8

12

1 *am forsworn* i.e. have violated my marriage vows   **3** *bed-vow* marriage
vows; *new faith torn* i.e. a new contract of fidelity torn up   **4** *bearing* i.e.
professing   **7** *but to misuse* i.e. merely to misrepresent   **11** *enlighten*
brighten; *gave . . . blindness* i.e. made the eyes swear to things they did not
see   **12** *swear against* i.e. falsely deny   **13** *eye* eyes (with a pun on *I*, cf.
ll. 11–12)

153

Cupid laid by his brand and fell asleep:
A maid of Dian's this advantage found
And his love-kindling fire did quickly steep
In a cold valley-fountain of that ground;   4
Which borrowed from this holy fire of Love
A dateless lively heat, still to endure,
And grew a seething bath, which yet men prove
Against strange maladies a sovereign cure.   8
But at my mistress' eye Love's brand new-fired,
The boy for trial needs would touch my breast;
I, sick withal, the help of bath desired
And thither hied, a sad distempered guest,   12
    But found no cure: the bath for my help lies
      Where Cupid got new fire, my mistress' eyes.

1 *brand* torch **2** *Dian* Diana, goddess of chastity; *advantage* opportunity
4 *of that ground* i.e. nearby **6** *dateless* eternal; *still* always **7** *grew* became;
yet to this day **10** *for . . . would* as an experiment had to **11** *withal* there-
from **12** *distempered* diseased

154

The little Love-god, lying once asleep,
Laid by his side his heart-inflaming brand,
Whilst many nymphs that vowed chaste life to keep
4   Came tripping by; but in her maiden hand
The fairest votary took up that fire
Which many legions of true hearts had warmed;
And so the general of hot desire
8   Was, sleeping, by a virgin hand disarmed.
This brand she quenchèd in a cool well by,
Which from Love's fire took heat perpetual,
Growing a bath and healthful remedy
12   For men diseased; but I, my mistress' thrall,
     Came there for cure, and this by that I prove:
     Love's fire heats water, water cools not love.

5 *votary* votaress (nymph of Diana) 7 *general* commander (Cupid)
9 *by* nearby 12 *thrall* slave

The parts of Sonnets 153 and 154 having to do with the creation of a hot bath by means of the quenching of Cupid's torch are variations upon a theme treated in various earlier epigrams, including one in fifth-century Greek by Marianus Scholasticus. These sonnets seem detached from the rest of the sequence, and their authenticity has been questioned.

INDEX OF FIRST LINES

INDEX OF FIRST LINES
The figures in parentheses refer to the number of the sonnet

A woman's face, with Nature's own hand painted (20)
Accuse me thus, that I have scanted all (117)
Against my love shall be as I am now (63)
Against that time, if ever that time come (49)
Ah, wherefore with infection should he live (67)
Alack, what poverty my Muse brings forth (103)
Alas, 'tis true I have gone here and there (110)
As a decrepit father takes delight (37)
As an unperfect actor on the stage (23)
As fast as thou shalt wane, so fast thou grow'st (11)

Be wise as thou art cruel: do not press (140)
Being your slave, what should I do but tend (57)
Beshrew that heart that makes my heart to groan (133)
Betwixt mine eye and heart a league is took (47)
But be contented: when that fell arrest (74)
But do thy worst to steal thyself away (92)
But wherefore do not you a mightier way (16)

Canst thou, O cruel, say I love thee not (149)
Cupid laid by his brand and fell asleep (153)

Devouring Time, blunt thou the lion's paws (19)

Farewell: thou art too dear for my possessing (87)
For shame, deny that thou bear'st love to any (10)
From fairest creatures we desire increase (1)
From you have I been absent in the spring (98)
Full many a glorious morning have I seen (33)

How can I then return in happy plight (28)
How can my Muse want subject to invent (38)
How careful was I, when I took my way (48)
How heavy do I journey on the way (50)

How like a winter hath my absence been (97)
How oft, when thou, my music, music play'st (128)
How sweet and lovely dost thou make the shame (95)

I grant thou wert not married to my Muse (82)
I never saw that you did painting need (83)
If my dear love were but the child of state (124)
If the dull substance of my flesh were thought (44)
If there be nothing new, but that which is (59)
If thou survive my well-contented day (32)
If thy soul check thee that I come so near (136)
In faith, I do not love thee with mine eyes (141)
In loving thee thou know'st I am forsworn (152)
In the old age black was not counted fair (127)
Is it for fear to wet a widow's eye (9)
Is it thy will thy image should keep open (61)

Let me confess that we two must be twain (36)
Let me not to the marriage of true minds (116)
Let not my love be called idolatry (105)
Let those who are in favor with their stars (25)
Like as the waves make towards the pebbled shore (60)
Like as to make our appetites more keen (118)
Lo, as a careful housewife runs to catch (143)
Lo, in the orient when the gracious light (7)
Look in thy glass, and tell the face thou viewest (3)
Lord of my love, to whom in vassalage (26)
Love is my sin, and thy dear virtue hate (142)
Love is too young to know what conscience is (151)

Mine eye and heart are at a mortal war (46)
Mine eye hath played the painter and hath stelled (24)
Music to hear, why hear'st thou music sadly (8)
My glass shall not persuade me I am old (22)
My love is as a fever, longing still (147)
My love is strength'ned, though more weak in seeming (102)

My mistress' eyes are nothing like the sun (130)
My tongue-tied Muse in manners holds her still (85)

No longer mourn for me when I am dead (71)
No more be grieved at that which thou hast done (35)
No, Time, thou shalt not boast that I do change (123)
Not from the stars do I my judgment pluck (14)
Not marble nor the gilded monuments (55)
Not mine own fears, nor the prophetic soul (107)

O, call not me to justify the wrong (139)
O, for my sake do you with Fortune chide (111)
O, from what pow'r hast thou this pow'rful might (150)
O, how I faint when I of you do write (80)
O, how much more doth beauty beauteous seem (54)
O, how thy worth with manners may I sing (39)
O, lest the world should task you to recite (72)
O me, what eyes hath Love put in my head (148)
O, never say that I was false of heart (109)
O, that you were yourself, but, love, you are (13)
O thou, my lovely boy, who in thy power (126)
O truant Muse, what shall be thy amends (101)
Or I shall live your epitaph to make (81)
Or whether doth my mind, being crowned with you (114)

Poor soul, the center of my sinful earth (146)

Say that thou didst forsake me for some fault (89)
Shall I compare thee to a summer's day (18)
Sin of self-love possesseth all mine eye (62)
Since brass, nor stone, nor earth, nor boundless sea (65)
Since I left you, mine eye is in my mind (113)
So am I as the rich whose blessèd key (52)
So are you to my thoughts as food to life (75)
So is it not with me as with that Muse (21)
So, now I have confessed that he is thine (134)
So oft have I invoked thee for my Muse (78)

So shall I live, supposing thou art true (93)
Some glory in their birth, some in their skill (91)
Some say thy fault is youth, some wantonness (96)
Sweet love, renew thy force; be it not said (56)

Take all my loves, my love, yea, take them all (40)
That god forbid that made me first your slave (58)
That thou art blamed shall not be thy defect (70)
That thou hast her, it is not all my grief (42)
That time of year thou mayst in me behold (73)
That you were once unkind befriends me now (120)
Th' expense of spirit in a waste of shame (129)
The forward violet thus did I chide (99)
The little Love-god, lying once asleep (154)
The other two, slight air and purging fire (45)
Then hate me when thou wilt; if ever, now (90)
Then let not winter's ragged hand deface (6)
They that have pow'r to hurt and will do none (94)
Thine eyes I love, and they, as pitying me (132)
Those hours that with gentle work did frame (5)
Those lines that I before have writ do lie (115)
Those lips that Love's own hand did make (145)
Those parts of thee that the world's eye doth view (69)
Those pretty wrongs that liberty commits (41)
Thou art as tyrannous, so as thou art (131)
Thou blind fool, Love, what dost thou to mine eyes (137)
Thus can my love excuse the slow offense (51)
Thus is his cheek the map of days outworn (68)
Thy bosom is endearèd with all hearts (31)
Thy gift, thy tables, are within my brain (122)
Thy glass will show thee how thy beauties wear (77)
Tired with all these, for restful death I cry (66)
'Tis better to be vile than vile esteemed (121)
To me, fair friend, you never can be old (104)
Two loves I have, of comfort and despair (144)

Unthrifty loveliness, why dost thou spend (4)

Was it the proud full sail of his great verse (86)
Weary with toil, I haste me to my bed (27)
Were't aught to me I bore the canopy (125)
What is your substance, whereof are you made (53)
What potions have I drunk of Siren tears (119)
What's in the brain that ink may character (108)
When forty winters shall besiege thy brow (2)
When I consider everything that grows (15)
When I do count the clock that tells the time (12)
When I have seen by Time's fell hand defaced (64)
When, in disgrace with Fortune and men's eyes (29)
When in the chronicle of wasted time (106)
When most I wink, then do mine eyes best see (43)
When my love swears that she is made of truth (138)
When thou shalt be disposed to set me light (88)
When to the sessions of sweet silent thought (30)
Where art thou, Muse, that thou forget'st so long (100)
Whilst I alone did call upon thy aid (79)
Who is it that says most, which can say more (84)
Who will believe my verse in time to come (17)
Whoever hath her wish, thou hast thy Will (135)
Why didst thou promise such a beauteous day (34)
Why is my verse so barren of new pride (76)

Your love and pity doth th' impression fill (112)

A selection of books published by Penguin is listed on the following pages.

For a complete list of books available from Penguin in the United States, write to Dept. DG, Penguin Books, 299 Murray Hill Parkway, East Rutherford, New Jersey 07073.

For a complete list of books available from Penguin in Canada, write to Penguin Books Canada Limited, 2801 John Street, Markham, Ontario L3R 1B4.

The Complete Pelican
SHAKESPEARE

To fill the need for a convenient and authoritative one-volume edition, the thirty-eight books in the Pelican series have been brought together.

THE COMPLETE PELICAN SHAKESPEARE includes all the material contained in the separate volumes, together with a 50,000-word General Introduction and full bibliographies. It contains the first nineteen pages of the First Folio in reduced facsimile, five new drawings, and illustrated endpapers. $9\frac{3}{4} \times 7\frac{3}{16}$ inches, 1520 pages.

INTRODUCING
SHAKESPEARE
Third Edition

G. B. Harrison

Now a classic, this volume has been the best popular in-
troduction to Shakespeare for over thirty years. Dr. G. B.
Harrison discusses first Shakespeare's legend and then his
tantalizingly ill-recorded life. Harrison describes the Eliza-
bethan playhouse (with the help of a set of graphic recon-
structions) and examines the effect of its complicated
structure on the plays themselves. It is in the chapter on
the Lord Chamberlain's Players that Shakespeare and his
associates are most clearly seen against their background
of theatrical rivalry, literary piracy, the closing of the play-
houses because of the plague, the famous performance of
Richard II in support of the Earl of Essex, and the fire that
finally destroyed the Globe Theater.

THE PENGUIN ENGLISH LIBRARY

The Penguin English Library Series reproduces, in convenient but authoritative editions, many of the greatest classics in English literature from Elizabethan times through the nineteenth century. Each volume is introduced by a critical essay, enhancing the understanding and enjoyment of the work for the student and general reader alike. A few selections from the list of more than one hundred titles follow:

PERSUASION, *Jane Austen*

PRIDE AND PREJUDICE, *Jane Austen*

SENSE AND SENSIBILITY, *Jane Austen*

JANE EYRE, *Charlotte Brontë*

WUTHERING HEIGHTS, *Emily Brontë*

THE WAY OF ALL FLESH, *Samuel Butler*

THE WOMAN IN WHITE, *Wilkie Collins*

GREAT EXPECTATIONS, *Charles Dickens*

HARD TIMES, *Charles Dickens*

MIDDLEMARCH, *George Eliot*

TOM JONES, *Henry Fielding*

WIVES AND DAUGHTERS, *Elizabeth Gaskell*

MOBY DICK, *Herman Melville*

THE SCIENCE FICTION OF EDGAR ALLAN POE

VANITY FAIR, *William Makepeace Thackeray*

CAN YOU FORGIVE HER?, *Anthony Trollope*

PHINEAS FINN, *Anthony Trollope*

THE NATURAL HISTORY OF SELBORNE, *Gilbert White*

THE PENGUIN BOOK OF
ELIZABETHAN VERSE

Edited by Edward Lucie-Smith

This extremely rich anthology includes not only poems by great poets like Thomas Campion, Thomas Dekker, Arthur Golding, and Shakespeare but also work by many less-famous men. Extraordinary variety appears in the editor's selections because the word *Elizabethan*, instead of referring to a style, is interpreted here as encompassing "poets whose reputations were made or largely sustained during the reign of Elizabeth." Edward Lucie-Smith is the editor of *British Poetry since 1945*, also published by Penguin Books.

Also available from Penguin Books

THE METAPHYSICAL POETS
Introduced and edited by Helen Gardner

THE PENGUIN BOOK OF BALLADS
Introduced and edited by Geoffrey Grigson

**THE PENGUIN BOOK OF
ENGLISH ROMANTIC VERSE**
Introduced and edited by David Wright

THE PENGUIN BOOK OF LOVE POETRY
Introduced and edited by Jon Stallworthy

**SCOTTISH LOVE POEMS:
A PERSONAL ANTHOLOGY**
Edited by Antonia Fraser

THE COMPLETE PLAYS

Christopher Marlowe
Edited by J. B. Steane

In recent years there has been a widening of opinion about Christopher Marlowe; at one extreme he is considered an atheist rebel and at the other, a Christian traditionalist. There is as much divergence in Marlowe's seven plays, and, as J. B. Steane says in his Introduction, that a man's work should encompass the extremes of *Tamburlaine* and *Edward the Second* is one of the most absorbingly interesting facts of literature. The range of Marlowe's small body of work covers such amazingly unlike pieces as *Doctor Faustus* and *The Jew of Malta*. Controlled and purposeful, these plays contain a poetry that enchants and lodges in the mind.

THREE PLAYS
THE WHITE DEVIL, THE DUCHESS OF MALFI, THE DEVIL'S LAW-CASE

John Webster
Introduction and Notes by David C. Gunby

In calling John Webster the "Tussaud Laureate" Bernard Shaw spoke for all the critics who have complained of the atmosphere of charnel house and torture chamber in Webster's plays. Certainly he can be morbid, macabre, and melodramatic, and he exploits to the full the theatrical possibilities of cruelty and violent death. Critics have too often identified Webster's views with those of his characters, however, and neglected his superb poetry and excellent craftsmanship. Though he was writing at a time of social confusion and pessimism, it is possible to see his own universe as an essentially moral one and his vision as deeply religious. On the evidence of the three plays in this volume, Webster can surely be regarded as a great poet and second only to Shakespeare as an English tragedian.

SHAKESPEARE

Anthony Burgess

Bare entries in parish registers, a document or two, and a
few legends and contemporary references make up the
known life of William Shakespeare. Anthony Burgess has
clothed these attractively with an extensive knowledge of
Elizabethan and Jacobean England for this elaborately
illustrated biography. The characters of the men Shake-
speare knew, the influence of his life on his plays, and the
stirring events that must have been in the minds of author,
actors, and audience are engagingly described here by a
writer who sees "Will" not as an ethereal bard but as a
sensitive, sensual, and shrewd man from the provinces
who turned his art to fortune in the most exciting years
of England's history. "It was a touch of near genius to
choose Mr. Burgess to write the text for a richly illustrated
life of Shakespeare, for his wonderfully well-stocked mind
and essentially wayward spirit are just right for summon-
ing up an apparition of the bard which is more convincing
than most"—David Holloway, *London Daily Telegraph*.
With 48 plates in color and nearly 100 black-and-white
illustrations.

THREE JACOBEAN TRAGEDIES

Edited by Gāmini Salgādo

Renaissance humanism had reached a crisis by the early seventeenth century. It was followed by a period of mental unrest, a sense of moral corruption and ambiguity which provoked the Jacobean dramatists to embittered satire and images of tragic retribution. John Webster in *The White Devil* paints a sinister and merciless world ruled by all the refinements of cunning and intrigue. In *The Revenger's Tragedy,* one of the most powerful of the Jacobean tragedies, Cyril Tourneur displays in a macabre ballet the emotional conflicts and vices typical of the age. *The Changeling* is perhaps the supreme achievement of Thomas Middleton—a masterpiece of brooding intensity.

FOUR JACOBEAN CITY COMEDIES

Edited by Gāmini Salgādo

The idiom of these Jacobean comedies is everywhere that of the bustling and bawdy metropolis, and the gulling of dupes and the seduction of women and the activities of sharpers and rogues are presented with irresistible vivacity. London and its court appeared to these dramatists as a striking and comprehensive image of human appetite and folly. Although satire may dominate, the moralist's censure is often tempered by an affection for the richness and variety of city life. Only Philip Massinger in *A New Way to Pay Old Debts,* his finest play, explicitly condemns human weakness. Both John Marston (*The Dutch Courtesan*) and Ben Jonson (*The Devil Is an Ass*), in expansive mood, remind us that man is also an animal and that he forgets this at his peril. In Thomas Middleton's *A Mad World, My Masters* we find an unambiguous celebration of the virtuosity of its villain-heroes.

PLAYS BY BERNARD SHAW

ANDROCLES AND THE LION

THE APPLE CART

ARMS AND THE MAN

BACK TO METHUSELAH

CAESAR AND CLEOPATRA

CANDIDA

THE DEVIL'S DISCIPLE

THE DOCTOR'S DILEMMA

HEARTBREAK HOUSE

MAJOR BARBARA

MAN AND SUPERMAN

THE MILLIONAIRESS

PLAYS UNPLEASANT
(WIDOWERS' HOUSES, THE PHILANDERER,
MRS WARREN'S PROFESSION)

PYGMALION

SAINT JOAN

SELECTED ONE ACT PLAYS
(THE SHEWING-UP OF BLANCO POSNET,
HOW HE LIED TO HER HUSBAND, O'FLAHERTY V.C.,
THE INCA OF PERUSALEM, ANNAJANSKA, VILLAGE WOOING,
THE DARK LADY OF THE SONNETS, OVERRULED,
GREAT CATHERINE, AUGUSTUS DOES HIS BIT,
THE SIX OF CALAIS)